Kitty Valentine
Dates an Actor

Spin the wheel.

jilliandodd

JILLIAN DODD

Jillian Dodd, Inc.
Madeira Beach, FL
Jillian Dodd, The Keatyn Chronicles, and Spy Girl are registered trademarks of Jillian Dodd, Inc.

Editor: Jovana Shirley, Unforeseen Editing,
www.unforeseenediting.com

ISBN: 978-1-953071-01-9

Books by Jillian Dodd

London Prep
London Prep: Book One
London Prep: Book Two
London Prep: Book Three

The Keatyn Chronicles
Stalk Me
Kiss Me
Date Me
Love Me
Adore Me
Hate Me
Get Me
Fame
Power
Money
Sex
Love
Keatyn Unscripted
Aiden

Kitty Valentine Series
*Kitty Valentine
dates a Billionaire*
*Kitty Valentine
dates a Doctor*
*Kitty Valentine
dates a Rockstar*
*Kitty Valentine
dates a Fireman*
*Kitty Valentine
dates an Actor*

That Boy Series
That Boy
That Wedding
That Baby
That Love
That Ring
That Summer

Spy Girl Series
The Prince
The Eagle
The Society
The Valiant
The Dauntless
The Phoenix
The Echelon

Love Series
Vegas Love
Broken Love
Fake Love

Girl off the Grid

Chapter One

"KITTY VALENTINE, WE need to talk about a few things," my editor, Maggie, says when I answer the phone.

This can't be good.

"Should I be sitting down?"

"No. No, it's not that serious."

Whew.

"The publisher has gotten backlogged from the holidays and doesn't have a place for you on the calendar right now."

"What? I thought you said it wasn't serious. I thought I was doing well. Selling books. Hitting lists. How can they not want me on the calendar? I need to talk to Lois. She'll fix this. I can't believe she didn't tell me all this. What about my contract?"

"Kitty, let me finish. There is no reason to bring your agent into this. We very much want you, but we have to wait for some books to go to print before we can put you on. You have a job. We still want your books. And honestly, if you can make them even hotter, the better."

"Maggie—"

"Don't start. You have made a vast improvement. I'm just saying, a girl likes it hot sometimes, so don't hold back on the next book."

"And when exactly will that be?"

"I don't know yet, but I want you to keep writing and keep going out. You'll just be that much further ahead when we can get you on the calendar."

I let out a long sigh. Thankfully, my job is secure. It's just weird since they were rushing my books out the door last year, and now, I don't know what to do with this downtime. If I'm being honest, I kinda liked the new schedule with tighter deadlines.

"Okay, I can do that. Is there anything else?"

"Yes."

I hold my breath. *What is it this time? Are my heroes not heroic enough? Not sexy enough? Not alpha enough?* I mean, it's not like I've been sitting around, making notes of all the possible weak points in my writing, but every author has a secret mental list just poised to explode at the slightest hint of criticism.

"I think you should take this time to also increase your online social presence. You have a Facebook page, but we need more from you. We need you to engage your readers. Let them get to know you. Especially the new you."

"Maggie, I thought that was something you all did."

"Yes, well, some self-promotion doesn't hurt. Readers today want to know the author. They want to think you're friends. And you know what? Friends buy their friend's books!"

"I'm not sure you're aware, but I'm a terribly boring person. When I'm not writing, I stay home. And I like it."

"Kitty, I know you feel like you're nothing without your work, but try to have a social life on- and off-line."

"Okay, what should I do?"

"Start making posts on Facebook since you already have a few followers there. Ask questions. Tell stories. Then, get on all the other outlets. Twitter, Instagram, Snapchat … heck, ask the readers what their favorites are and post there."

"And how does one do that and write and date, all at the same time?"

"Kitty, seriously, it's not that hard. Now, go figure it out and let me know who your next book will be about. I've got to run to a meeting. Oh, and, Kitty? I'll be watching."

That's not creepy at all.

I plop onto the couch with a huff after she hangs up. I can't wait to tell Hayley all about this at dinner tonight. Maybe my best friend will take pity on me and tell me how to get on Snapagram, or whatever it's called, and what to do once I'm on there.

Jeez. I sound like an old lady.

Thankfully, the heart-shaped box of chocolates I

bought earlier on an impulse is sitting within reach. I tear off the wrapper and shove a piece into my mouth.

Mmhmm ... buttercream ... take me away.

Chapter Two

"WHO'S THAT GORGEOUS lady?" Hayley's laughing as she stands to give me a hug when I finally make it through the crowd by the front door to where she's already waiting at a corner table. I put the bag I'm holding down and hug her back.

"You like?"

"Yeah." She gives me an approving look as she sits. "You look terrific. Is that new?"

I run a hand over the front of my dress. "Yes. I got it online during an after-Christmas sale."

"I want one for myself."

"Hmm. Funny you should say that." I nudge the bag at my feet in her direction.

"You didn't."

"Maybe I did." It's hard not to burst out laughing as I take a seat across from her.

Her eyes light up as she bends to go through the tissue paper. "You did!"

"Happy New Year! Now, we can be twins sometime. I'm sure you'll drag me somewhere fabulous to wear them to."

She pulls it out of the bag to admire it. "I can't

wait to try it on the second I get home."

"It should fit. It's true to size. But I put a gift receipt in there, just in case."

"You think of everything." She's shaking her head while folding the dress to put it back in the bag. "You're the best." She lifts her glass of wine in my direction. "And you're the best friend ever too."

"Ditto." I pour a glass from the bottle sitting in a bucket beside the table. "So, I got a call from Maggie today."

"Is it time to pick your new man? I brought the spinner hoping it was."

It's amazing, the way her eyes light up. I don't know what I did to deserve such an amazing friend; I really don't.

"Yes, but ..."

"Uh-oh, what is it?"

"There's a backlog of books, and I'm not on the schedule."

"Then, why are we picking a new guy? I don't understand."

"They still want me, and Maggie wants me to keep working, so my book will be ready by the time I get on the schedule."

"Is that normal?"

"Apparently, it can happen. When I was only writing one or two books a year, it didn't really matter. Now that I've been churning them out, it's part of my new normal, I guess."

"Well, that's good news. Why don't you look

happy about it?"

"She said I also have to increase my social media presence."

Before she has the chance to ask what the heck I'm talking about, our server appears. "Hello, ladies." He smiles, all sweetness and warmth. "I hope you had a wonderful holiday season. Happy New Year."

"Thanks." Hayley tosses her glossy blonde hair over one shoulder. "Thought I'd take the old ball and chain out for a night on the town."

"Shut up." I laugh.

"You make a gorgeous couple," he assures us with a wink before placing a basket of warm bread and a bowl of fancy olive oil on the table. "What would you like to order?"

Hayley speaks up, "She'll have the shrimp scampi, and I'll have the mushroom ravioli."

He writes down our orders and is gone before I can tell him we're not a couple.

"We might as well be," Hayley reasons as she drags her bread through the fragrant oil. "This is the longest relationship I've ever been in, and I like you better than just about anybody else in the world."

"Thanks for that. Ditto, by the way."

"And I never have to wonder if you're gonna ghost me."

"You'd find me. I mean, you know where I live, and you know I'm too set in my ways to ever move."

"That's true. They'll have to drag you out, kicking and screaming, one day. Or you know, dead."

"Such romantic talk from my pretend girlfriend."

Her perfectly arched brows lift. "Speaking of relationships …"

I can't help but rub my hands together in anticipation. "Yes, ma'am. I guess we'd better get this part over with, huh?"

Hayley shoots me a skeptical look as she pulls the spinner from her purse. "Who are you, and what did you do with Kitty? You're never raring to go when it comes time to pull out the old spinner."

"I'm not usually dying to get some work done. I don't want to lose momentum. I need something to occupy my brain or else it starts getting all hectic up here." I tap my temple.

"Yeah. I've seen what happens when things get crazy up in there. Remember that time the building's power went out and your laptop battery died and you cut your bangs by candlelight?"

"You swore to never speak of that," I whisper, eyes narrowed.

"It took forever for them to grow out."

"I'm going to take that dress back."

"No!" She pulls the bag away from me with a laugh. "You'll have to pry it out of my cold, dead hands."

"Then, let us never speak of Bangsgate again."

"I promise." She points to the spinner with one freshly manicured blood-red nail. "Let's see who it is this time."

"Oh, what's that?" our server interrupts us as he sets a tray down on one of those folding stands.

Wow, that was quick.

Hayley beats me to the explanation. "It's a spinner. It'll tell her who she has to date next."

Poor guy. He's more than a little confused. "Excuse me?"

Granted, it was none of his business in the first place, but still, I feel like I should clarify. "I'm a writer, looking to date somebody new for my next book. This device tells me the sort of person I have to look for."

"Oh. I thought you two were a couple." He slides a plate of shrimp scampi in front of me. "I mean, when your friend ordered for you …"

"She knows what I like." And I do love the shrimp scampi here. Why not overload on garlic tonight? It's not like I'm going to be kissing anybody.

Not that I'm bitter about that or anything. I just wasn't the right girl for my previous dates.

"So, you aren't a couple?" he asks, and naturally, his attention shifts solely to Hayley. "Does that mean you're single?"

Her smile is warm as she explains, "I am, but I'm also a lawyer who works eighty hours a week. This is a rare night out."

"Gotcha." After asking whether we need anything else, he takes his tray and his stand and what's left of his pride, and he hurries away.

"You know—and I'm not complaining when I say this—every time I'm with you, it's like I become invisible."

She shrugs it off like it hasn't happened a hundred times before, digging into her mushroom ravioli. "He knew you were gonna be dating somebody soon."

And I swear, it sounds like she actually means it. Like she has no idea how absolutely stunning and magnetic she is.

"Yeah. I'm sure that's it." With that, I give the spinner a spin. "Let's see who I'm going after this time."

"You make it sound so fun and romantic." She reaches across the table and spears a shrimp in time to avoid being stabbed in the hand. By me.

We both stare at the small opening and watch the various types of men go past. All the most popular tropes in romance, minus the ones I notice Hayley has crossed out. Even without billionaire, boss, doctor, rock star, and firefighter, there are still plenty to choose from.

Including the one left showing through the plastic screen once the spinner stops.

Hayley lets out a tiny squeal. "Actor! Yay!"

"What's so exciting about that?"

"Um, hello, we live in New York. You can't

swing a dead cat without finding an actor. Hell, our server's probably an actor. You should ask him."

"When he forgot I existed a minute ago? No, thanks. I do have at least a scrap of self-respect."

"Fine then. I wonder how you can find an actor."

"Besides swinging a dead cat?" I stick my tongue out when she gives me a sour look. "Actually, I think maybe I can find a way. Though it'll take a minute. Huh. I wonder …"

"What is it?"

I have to hold up a finger to shush her since an idea is brewing in my head and it might be pretty big. "I wonder if I could find one on social media," I finally suggest before chewing my lip. "Is that a terrible idea?"

"Not terrible. Just … surprising."

"Right. I didn't get to finish telling you what Maggie said about me building more of an audience. I have to spend more time on social media and, like, build my platform or something. Whatever it is she said."

"It makes sense. All writers should have a presence."

"Don't get me started. Back to the matter at hand. I could always send feelers out on social media, right? If Maggie thinks it's okay, I mean. Like if I announce my newest book's theme and ask if there are any actors in the area who'd be willing to get together and answer questions. It doesn't have to be presented as a date thing. But it could turn into that if I liked the guy and there was … you know … a spark."

"I think you're a freaking genius."

"I thought that was already an agreed-upon thing."

"Oh, right. I forgot."

She tries to spear another shrimp, but I'm too fast for her this time.

"Girl, if you don't think I'll stab you in front of all these people …" I jab my fork in her direction just in case she decides not to take me seriously.

"So, let me get this straight. They want you to up your presence on social media while you're waiting to get on the schedule?"

"I guess it's something I should've been doing all along. I wish somebody had told me. Have I been too much of a hermit all this time?"

"I think I already told you that … back in October. And seriously, how are you not already on social media?"

"Remind me why we're friends again," I mutter.

"Because if you didn't have me, you'd never go anywhere. Besides, social media should be right up your alley. You can talk to people without going out."

"You do have a point."

"I know. Plus, there are so many writers out there. Have you ever considered joining a writing group? Like, to critique and encourage each other?

To bounce ideas? You never know what you could learn until you try."

I have to resist the impulse to bury my head in my arms on the table. Mostly because this is a nice restaurant and there's a plate of food in front of me. It's one thing for my breath to smell like garlic and another for my hair to be dripping with garlic butter. I didn't take the time to curl it for that to happen.

"Is it like this for lawyers?" I ask, just a little unhappy.

"What's that mean?"

"Are you always being told there's more you should be doing? More to learn, more to keep on top of?"

"Um, yeah. The law isn't set in place. It's always changing with new rulings and statutes. We have to keep up with the revisions, and it's a lot of work."

"So, in other words, the fact that I haven't done any of these things doesn't mean I'm the world's worst writer?"

"It doesn't make you the world's worst writer. Not even the second or third worst. So, don't worry about it. You've gotten by so far, and you could probably still get by without them."

She leans in a little, looking me straight in the eye. "But do you want to? Or do you wanna continue stretching yourself as a writer? It's your craft, right? It's what you do. It's your life. You might as well learn as much about it as you can.

And, hey, maybe you'll meet a bunch of people who will never be as cool as me but are still pretty cool."

That is why Hayley is my date tonight. She's the best.

"I don't know if anybody could ever be as cool as you, so you don't have to worry about it."

"Don't forget that and end up getting a bunch of new writer friends and ignore me."

"That would never happen."

Our server pops over with a wink for Hayley. "How's everything over here?"

"Great." She smiles at me. "And we found out my friend is going to date an actor next."

Big surprise, he suddenly notices I'm sitting here. "An actor? Hey, I'm an actor."

"I should've put money on it," Hayley whispers.

Chapter Three

"LET ME GET this straight."

I roll my eyes until they're practically falling out of my head. "Why do I tell you anything?"

"Because I ask—and that's because it's always fun to hear about your new victim." Matt tips his head back, tossing a dumpling in the air and catching it in his open mouth.

"That's a good way to choke to death. Not that I'd mind it if you did."

"Please. What would you do without me? I shudder to think."

"I did pretty well without you for about twenty-four years, thanks."

"That's up for debate."

He hands a piece of chicken to Phoebe, his beautiful golden retriever, who I like a lot more than I like him. If dogs could smile, she'd be beaming from ear to ear. Only the way he looks at her keeps me from stabbing him the way I threatened to stab Hayley during dinner last night.

He loves her and spoils her rotten, which is at least a point in his favor. He might have a soul.

"Anyway," he continues when he turns my way again, "you're gonna date an actor this time."

"Yes."

"Who you plan to meet online. Are you using that dating profile again?"

My cheeks flush, and I really wish I could control them better because they make me look like I'm guilty of something. "No. I'm not using it. I probably should've deleted it after meeting Jake."

As it turned out, my dating profile hadn't led me to Jake, the sexy ER doc who whispered his ex-girlfriend's name while naked in my bed. Right before we almost … you know.

It was Phoebe—currently sniffing my tofu and spring rolls—who made me sprain my ankle on the stairs. All it took was getting wrapped up in a leash and dragged to the ER by Matt.

"Or—and this is just a wacky idea that popped into my head—you could use it to actually date people. Not strictly for work stuff." His eyes widen. "Shocking, I know."

I have to raise my voice to shut him up. "Anyway, like I was saying, this will be via social media. I have to get online and make friendly with people."

"You don't have a social media presence?"

He gets a look for that one.

"Why do you make it sound like I just admitted I don't wash my feet in the shower?"

"Do you?"

"Yes, of course. I'm not an animal. I can't believe

you'd even ask me that. And now, I'm starting to feel like you don't."

"I do." But he won't maintain eye contact. "Anyway, I was surprised because everybody has a social media presence nowadays. Especially artists, people in the public eye, entertainers."

"I've always done well enough without it." I shrug. "I didn't think it was such a big deal. Obviously, if the publisher had brought this up before, I would've done something about it. Maybe they did and just thought I was being difficult when I didn't do it. I don't remember. I was trying to write."

"What are you going to do now?"

"I guess do what they want me to do, like I did when we started this whole new sexy-books thing."

"Eh, you'll be fine. Although ..." He frowns, going silent.

I shouldn't ask. I know I shouldn't ask. Curiosity killed the kitty and all that.

There's clearly a disconnect between my brain and my mouth, however. "Although what?" I ask when I can't take it anymore. "What is it?"

He shrugs, his frown deepening. "It's just that I'm not sure what you could do to keep your fans thinking you're a cool, normal person."

Which is why I shouldn't have asked. "I hate you."

"No, you don't. Or you wouldn't have offered to pick up the lunch tab today. What gives?" He pops another dumpling into his mouth, so smooth, so sure of himself.

Ugh, he's insufferable.

"I don't know. It's been a while since I've heard screaming emanating from your apartment. In fact, I haven't heard much of anything over there lately—though I do sometimes hear you coming in first thing in the morning. Not from a walk or a run with Phoebe since she doesn't scratch at my door."

"Detective Valentine." He snorts.

But, again, he won't meet my gaze, so I know something's up. He likes to pretend he thinks I'm useless and it doesn't matter what I say, but he's full of it. The second I hit on something, he clams right up and turns especially snarky.

"What's up? Are you moonlighting? Is being a financial wizard not as lucrative as it once was?"

His hazel eyes aren't sparkling with humor anymore. "Knock it off."

Now, you'd think I'd take this as a hint that I should indeed knock it off. But here's the thing: it's so rare for me to have him in this position—where I know there's something he'd rather I not know, therefore giving me a little bit of power over him—that it would be stupid of me to let this go. "Are you now a gentleman of the night? An escort for bored, wealthy, older women with questionable taste?"

At least that earns me a snicker.

"I think we both know they wouldn't have questionable taste, Valentine." He lifts and lowers his eyebrows, all suggestive-like.

"That's up for debate." It's not every day I get to throw his words back at him. Boy, this impromptu lunch was a great idea. I'm batting a thousand.

"Touché." He rolls his eyes before tossing Phoebe another piece of chicken from his chow mein. No matter how many times he orders it, I still think it's disgusting.

"For real. Come on. Believe it or not, I sort of care what happens to you."

He raises a skeptical brow to go along with his skeptical smirk. "Oh, really? That's news."

"Well, I mean, I'd have to take care of Phoebe if you kicked the bucket or went to jail or whatever. It would affect me."

"You think I'd give Phoebe to you? Please."

"What's wrong with me? Who the heck else would you give her to?"

"You're not the only person I know, Kitty." He rolls his eyes, which is a total me move.

There's definitely something going on.

"Where have you been lately? I won't stop asking until you tell me."

"It's none of—"

"Where've you been? Where've you been? Where've you been? Where've you been?"

He throws his hands into the air, red-faced. "Fine, I'm seeing someone! Okay?"

My mouth snaps shut. That's not what I was expecting. Not that I have any idea what I was expecting.

But that wasn't it.

He looks up at the ceiling with a sigh. "Now, you know. I'm seeing someone."

What am I supposed to say? Matt doesn't date people. He hooks up. At least, that's always been his method. I feel like somebody dropped me in the middle of an ice-cold pool.

"Oh. I, um, I don't know why I didn't think of that right away."

He chuckles before going back to his food. "Yeah, you do. We both know why you didn't. And you can make fun of me all you want but only for the length of time it takes to finish our lunch. After that, I don't want to hear anything about it."

"I wasn't going to make fun of you."

"Bullshit."

"Matt, I wasn't."

He glances up from his container. "You mean it?"

"Of course! I'm not like you."

"Really? How so?"

"I, for one, don't take perverse pleasure in tormenting people the way you take pleasure from tormenting me, you dork. Jeez." I look him up and down, biting back a smile. "Curiosity, on the other hand, that's my forte."

"I figured that was coming too."

"So … what's she like? What's her name? Where does she work? Where does she live?"

"Do you want to know her blood type too? Maybe the name of her childhood best friend?"

"Hey, I'm sorry for caring."

"You're being nosy. That's not the same as caring."

"Don't tell me how to care, Matt. And let us not forget that you've quizzed me on the guys I've dated recently. You knew just about everything about them, and don't even pretend like you didn't give me a ton of crap."

"All right." He leaves the container on the coffee table before rubbing his palms on his legs. Like he's nervous. "Her name is Gretchen. She's in my line of work. We met through a mutual friend last month."

"Last month?"

"Yeah."

"Last month?" That earns him a pillow to the side of the head. "You've been seeing somebody for weeks, and you didn't say anything? What the heck?"

"I don't know. Like I said, I expected you to make fun of me. And it's not like I expected it to last six weeks—"

"Six weeks? So, what, since before Christmas? Matt!"

"Okay, okay, I should've said something. Fine."

"Wow. No wonder I've hardly seen you around."

"Aw, did you miss me?"

"Clearly not, or I would've mentioned something about this before. Trust me, I've appreciated the peace and quiet. But you could've said something. That's all I'm trying to say."

"Point taken."

"If you ever plan on spending the night away and need somebody to look in on Phoebe, let me know."

"Will do."

"What's she like?"

"She's nice." He holds my gaze, chewing slowly and deliberately. "I don't wanna talk about it right now."

"Okay, fine. We'll talk about my life. Jeez. I thought, for once, you'd like to talk about yourself."

"Nope. I like talking about you a whole lot better. It takes the focus off me."

"And it gives you the opportunity to make fun of me."

"Ex-actly. So, an actor this time, huh? You think you can handle that?"

"Why would I not be able to?"

"Actors and their egos. You know how it is."

"That's not necessarily true. It's a stereotype."

"Stereotypes have to come from somewhere. So, it must've been true for somebody at some point. Just sayin'."

"I don't care. I'm going into this with an open mind. And, hey, if I put up with Dustin's ego, I can handle an actor. I even put up with your ego, which is seriously saying something."

"It's not all ego if it's true. At least I can back my ego up."

I won't even bother to dignify that one with a reply. "So, I'll announce on social media that I'd like to meet an actor and pick their brain for my next book. I already have a few hundred followers, so hopefully, they'll see what I post."

"Prepare yourself," he murmurs, picking at what's left of his food with his chopsticks.

"What's that mean?"

"It means, prepare yourself. Gird your loins and all that."

"Why?"

"You can't be this naive. Because the internet is full of disgusting trolls and jerks and people whose entire life's goal is to make the rest of the world as miserable as they are."

"Not my fans though."

"No, not your fans." He rolls his eyes, snickering. "It's not your fans who will be the problem. It's men in general. We're a bunch of pigs."

"You said it. Not me."

"Just wait and see how many dick pics you get."

"Ew, Matt."

"I'm just saying, prepare yourself."

I put the rest of my food aside, taking care to keep it out of Phoebe's reach. "Listen, I know you think I'm naive, but I'm a well-educated woman. Surely, I can handle myself on social media."

"Okay, but don't say I didn't warn you."

Chapter Four

HERE'S THE THING about me: I'm always writing checks my mouth can't cash.

It's been all of one day since I had that lunchtime conversation with Matt. One short day ago, I was so young and naive. Fresh-faced and full of confidence.

I'll never recapture that innocence. My innocence has been destroyed.

By dicks. By so many dicks.

Small dicks. Big, veiny dicks—turns out, I don't like them that way after all.

Dicks in just about every conceivable skin color. Some of them with a hand around their base, some standing on their own.

And I only asked less than twelve hours ago for my fans to reach out to any actors they know. Twelve hours is all it took for a deluge of unsolicited photos to pretty much flood my accounts.

"I'm drowning in dick pics," I moan to Hayley once I'm finally able to get her on the phone as she's leaving work for the night. This isn't the sort of thing I could adequately convey via text.

"Stop playing."

"*Glub, glub, glub.* That's the sound of me drowning. In dicks."

"Send in the lifeboat, Kitty is going down." There's barely suppressed laughter in her voice.

Okay, maybe that's a tiny bit funny. "You too? I don't know if I can handle two smarty-pants people in my life. There's a reason I'm not bothering to tell him about this."

"Matt was right then."

"Yeah, yeah, he was right. And whatever. Forget about him. I'm more concerned with the fact that there are, like, a hundred dicks for every one legitimate, helpful response."

"Sorry Kitty, but seriously delete and block. Delete and block. Over and over again. It's literally the only thing you can do to combat this."

"I'm supposed to be expanding my online presence. Is that what expanding my presence means? Spending hours blocking people for being idiots and gross pigs?"

"Probably, yeah. You should hire an assistant to do that for you."

"Yeesh. One hurdle at a time, lady."

Right now though, it's extremely tempting. If I could outsource dick pic deletion, I'd have it made.

"Did you at least get any solid leads?"

"Yeah. I have a few messages marked as being important, aka the messages I shouldn't delete. And they seem like actual, genuine messages written by true fans." I scroll through one of them and then another. "There are still fans out there who want to talk about real things. Not just their genitals."

"Humanity isn't completely going down the toilet then."

"It would look that way. What a relief."

"Are there at least any decent-looking dicks in your inbox?"

"Oh, gross."

"I'm just saying, there might be a few good ones in there. Dicks worth investigating."

"No freaking way."

"You're turning down an abundance of dicks? Just like that? When so many of us are dick-deprived?"

"I could forward the messages to you. And, hey, it's not like, if given the choice, every single one of the guys attached to them wouldn't choose you. Because they would."

"No, thank you. You're so generous, but I couldn't take those dicks from you. They're your dicks, Kitty."

"I'm dick-wealthy."

"You are." She giggles, finally breaking up her serious tone. "Men are disgusting."

"They really are. Why do we even let them live?"

"You think I haven't asked myself that question? I deal with more stuck-up, self-centered, mediocre men in a single day than you've ever dealt with in your entire life. It's disheartening."

"How do you deal with it?"

"I just do. I pull up my big girl panties and show them I'm more than a pretty face."

We share a quiet little laugh over that, but I know there's a lot of painful truth at the core of what she's saying. I joke about how beautiful Hayley is and how she overshadows me and just about everybody else in the room, no matter where she is or what she's doing.

The fact is, her looks have caused problems in the past. Not because she can't handle her beauty, but because other people can't. Like men in positions of power who think they can make jokes about her skirt length or the neckline of her blouse.

The girl is a certified genius, but that doesn't seem to be enough for them.

"So, it looks like I'll be meeting a few people for coffee this week. I have to admit, I have no idea how to get started with this. Am I burned out? Am I in a rut?"

"Meet your actor, or actors, or whoever. Maybe that will inspire you. And in the meantime, think up your sexier scenes. You can write them without knowing exactly what's happening in the rest of the book, can't you?"

"I mean, I guess I could. I've never tried that before."

I'm more of a linear writer. I don't know how a sex scene will unfold without knowing the characters.

But I could always go back in and tweak as necessary. The basic bones of the scene wouldn't have to change that much.

"I need sexy inspiration too," I admit.

"Afraid I can't help you there. Sorry about that."

"I'll try to forgive you."

"But don't worry. You have all those handsome, stately dicks to look at and ponder over."

There's no holding back the gag this inspires. "You wouldn't even joke like that if you had to look at some of them. The words *handsome* and *stately* don't come to mind; let's just put it that way."

"Thanks for making me laugh anyway," she sighs. The traffic noise in the background has faded, replaced by the weird echoing sound of her voice. She must be in her building now, on her way up the stairs. "Laughing is one thing I haven't done enough of lately."

"Just think how great life will be when all of this is behind you and you become partner," I suggest.

"That is years away."

"But knowing you, you'll find a way to hack it and make partner before you turn thirty."

"I wish I had your positive outlook. God, did I really just say that?" She laughs.

I try not to take offense—I mean, she's not wrong. I'm not always the most positive person. And I might or might not have a tendency to be a little … dramatic.

"Hey, one of the people who reached out—and who actually seems to be a decent person—invited me to an acting workshop on Friday night. You should come with me. It would be an excuse to be around people for a little while."

"I can't. I'm sorry," she adds when I groan. "I need to finish reviewing a contract."

"Of course you do. I shouldn't tempt you like that. Are you eating enough? Are you getting enough sleep?"

"I'm trying, Mom. And now, I have to heat up leftovers and look over some updated documents I just got."

I know there's a good reason for her to work this hard, but I can't help hating the fatigue in her voice. As soon as we're off the phone, I put in an order for a bunch of food to be delivered to her apartment. Even if she doesn't eat it tonight, she'll have it for when she comes home late the next few nights.

Now, all that's left to do is delete more dick pics and agree to visit the acting workshop. The girl who offered the invite is named Ashley, and she's posted tons of photos of her and her friends wearing costumes, getting made up in dressing rooms, goofing off onstage, and putting sets together.

It looks so darn fun!

"I would like to paint sets," I whisper, scrolling through her photos. "And go shopping for props in thrift stores."

Then again, there are lots of people who think

writing from home is super easy and fun too. I could tell them a few stories that would burst their bubbles.

Hi, Ashley! Thank you so much for reaching out with your generous offer, I type. I would love to visit your acting workshop this Friday and learn more about what it's like to be an actor.

No sooner do I send the message than there's a knock at my door.

"Freaky," I mutter as I get up from my desk to see who it is. Not that there are too many possibilities—we're not exactly neighborly in this building.

"Is it wrong that you're the only person in the building who I know by name?" I ask after swinging the door open to find Matt standing in front of me.

And oh goodness gracious, does he look good. It's easy to forget how fundamentally hot he is when he spends so much of his time generally acting like a pain in the butt.

With a rueful smile, he runs a hand through his freshly trimmed brown hair. "You're the only one I know by name. Hell, it's Manhattan. How many people know their neighbors? It took a year for us to finally start talking."

"Yeah, I remember those days. Good days. When I didn't know who you were and I had an inkling of self-esteem." I hold my thumb and forefinger an inch apart.

"Always the victim." He snickers. "So, listen, I'm on my way out, and I might be gone for the night. Would you make sure Phoebe gets walked before you go to bed tonight?"

"Sure. She could spend the night here with me, if you want," I offer. "She might get lonely over there by herself."

"I doubt it. She'll use this as an opportunity to stretch out on my bed. I don't crate her when I'm away for the night." He explains when I throw him a look of surprise, "It seems mean."

"Even so. Why do you think she sleeps on your bed? Not for physical comfort, dummy."

"And you're the one talking about me ruining your self-esteem?"

"Because she's lonely and she wants to be near something that smells like you. God, you're the worst."

He winces a little. "You think so? Now, I feel like shit."

"Okay, okay, you don't have to feel that bad. Jeez. But think of her. You're usually home with her all day. She doesn't understand why you've suddenly disappeared for the whole night."

"You're killing me." He turns back toward his apartment and goes inside. "Phoebe, baby, I'm sorry. I'm sorry, sweet girl."

Sure enough, when I follow him in, *I find Phoebe relaxing on his bed. Is she really doing it to wrap herself in his scent while he's gone? How would I know? But I'd* be willing to make a bet.

"I'll keep her with me overnight. You don't have to worry about her for a minute."

"Thank you." He looks back over his shoulder, kneeling next to the bed in a fabulous, perfectly tailored suit.

"And for heaven's sake, get off the floor in your nice pants. Do I have to tell you everything? Go, go, go be with your girlfriend or whatever you want to call her."

I take Phoebe by the collar and guide her from the apartment. She goes right across the hall and straight into mine before making herself comfy on the couch.

"What's that then?" he asks as he straightens himself out, brushing a few stray dog hairs from his knees. "Is she trying to get your scent on her?"

"Shush." I look him up and down, noting the silk tie, flashy watch, and shiny shoes. Jeez, I could probably count on both hands the number of times I've seen him in shoes and still have fingers left over.

"Do I pass muster?" he asks with a wry smirk.

"Honestly?"

"I would expect nothing less."

"Yeah, you pass. You look good, and you know it."

"I just wanted to hear it from you." He winks before turning away, and he whistles as he jogs down the stairs.

What's this feeling in my chest? This strange tightness, which also feels ever so slightly like disappointment? I guess maybe I'm feeling a little lonely right now.

Even though I'm not alone. There's a gorgeous blonde sacked out on my couch, waiting for belly rubs.

Who am I to refuse?

Chapter Five

OKAY, SO I might've expected a little more than this.

Which was a big mistake on my part. *Didn't I already learn from my experience with Dustin? He was a once-famous performer singing in dumps. What did I expect from random actors? Glamour?*

This place is anything but glamorous. It's a small little room with rows of chairs set up on all four sides. There's an empty square in the center, where I guess the actors will do their thing.

I should've asked Ashley exactly what I'd be seeing tonight.

I also should've asked Ashley where to find her. Maybe ten or fifteen people are milling around, chatting quietly like they know each other. None of them look anything like the girl whose profile picture I studied in advance of showing up here.

What can I say? I like to be prepared.

But there was no way to prepare myself for feeling like a fish out of water. I have no idea what to do with myself, so I decide to take a seat and send Ashley a message, saying I've arrived. After that, I look around. I study the space, the people, the feeling in the air.

It feels cold in here. That's the feeling. I'm glad I wore a scarf, which I now wish were thicker and longer, and maybe I should have worn a pair of gloves because my hands are freezing. I cross my arms and tuck them into my elbows to warm them up.

"Kitty?" A redheaded girl wearing a long black dress waves as she hurries across the stage. "Sorry. I think the heat went out today, and we can't get the landlord on the phone."

"Oh, it's okay." I laugh, even as I fight to keep my teeth from chattering. "Ashley, right?"

"That's right. Do you mind?" She holds her arms out for a hug. Her cheeks are flushed almost deeply enough to hide her freckles. "I've been a fan for so long."

"You have? That is so sweet." And it deserves a hug. At least she asked beforehand rather than tackling me. "I'm so happy you saw my post and responded. Thank you for that. It's nice to know somebody's out there and actually paying attention."

"Are you kidding?" She giggles, letting me go. "I mean, it was perfect. You were looking for actors. I'm an actor. All my friends are actors."

She's also incredibly jittery and excited, but maybe that has to do with the performance tonight. "So, what are you and your friends doing here? What are you performing?"

"We're doing short scenes we've been working on for the last few months. A handful of us are writers—nothing like you, of course," she adds with a nervous laugh. "Now, I'm starting to wonder if it was a good idea to have you here. You'll probably think we're a bunch of hacks who don't know how to string words together."

"I'm sure I won't. And don't forget, what you read from me goes through a couple of editors before it ever reaches you. I shudder to think about the feedback I'd get on my first drafts."

Ashley spots a pair of girls on the other side of the room and waves them over. Like her, they're dressed entirely in black. "This is Kitty! The writer I was telling you about. Kitty, this is Bianca and Madison."

Bianca carries herself like a dancer. I'd be surprised if she didn't study dance at some point. "Hi, it's so nice to meet you! I've seen Ashley carrying your books around so many times."

"Same here," Madison agrees with a grin. "I heard they've gotten a little sexier too. That might be enough to get me to read them."

"Yeah, they have. So, she told you I'm going to be writing about an actor this time?"

"Good luck, girl." Bianca rolls her eyes, scoffing a little. "I could tell you a few stories."

"Me too," Madison agrees, folding her arms in what looks like a defensive pose. "Egomaniacs."

"Guys are bad enough to begin with," Ashley

sighs. "But actors? They're, like, concentrated ego."

Well, this is promising.

"They can't be all that bad. There has to be good things about them too, right?"

"Penicillin is good, but it's also mold. And not all mold is penicillin." Bianca delivers this with all the gravitas of someone bestowing a piece of deep wisdom.

All I can do is nod slowly, like I understand.

I sure do wish Hayley had been able to come with me.

"Yo, Ash!" A guy also dressed in black waves to her from the door. "Got the landlord on the phone."

"Excuse me. Kitty, please, make yourself comfortable. We'll be starting soon, and I'll meet up with you afterward." Ashley jogs over to the door, leaving me with the girls.

"So, you're actresses, huh? And did either of you write a scene for tonight?"

They shake their heads.

"Actually, Rafael wrote the scene we're performing with him." Madison's voice takes on a softer tone when she says his name. Like she's talking about somebody important.

"Rafael's sort of the star of the group," Bianca informs me in case I didn't already pick it up. "He's even done off-Broadway. He was nominated for a Barrymore in Philly too."

I assume that's a big deal, so I act like it is. "Wow. Impressive."

"And he has an agent. An actual agent. Not somebody who operates out of the back of a Chinese restaurant, like I do." Bianca sighs, shrugging. "But what can you do?"

"I know all about agents," I assure her with a grimace. "I've been trying to get mine on the phone all week. I think she's avoiding me."

"Wow, are you sure we're not talking about the same person?" Then, Bianca notices somebody across the room and grabs Madison's arm. "Bill Watson's here. Let's go say hi."

Neither of them explains who Bill Watson is before they scurry off to chat with him, but that's okay. I'm a little overwhelmed—and not only because I so rarely venture out into the world. But also because there are so many large personalities in this small, windowless space.

The room's filling with people now, so I take my seat before somebody tries to take it for themselves. It seems to me that this Rafael person is the one I really want to make a point of getting to know. He's the serious actor in the group. He was nominated for an award even.

After looking it up on my phone, it's clear the Barrymore Award is an impressive accomplishment in Philadelphia theater. I wish I'd gotten Rafael's full name, so I could look him up too.

There's no time for that though since the lights go down over the audience and pick up over the area in the center of the room. A bunch of people stream out from the sides of the auditorium, carrying chairs—Ashley and her friends among them.

Which one is Rafael?

All the men are fit, good-looking, and have a type of physical presence that I guess an actor has to adopt. At first glance, I have to admit, I wouldn't kick any of them out of bed for eating crackers.

But there's one in particular who my gaze keeps returning to. There's just something about him. He's gorgeous, for one thing, with hair almost as blond as Hayley's. It sparkles under the lights trained on the stage—if it can be called a stage—and just barely skims his shoulders. His eyes are an icy blue and his full mouth gives me a multitude of sexy, dirty thoughts.

Something tells me I've found my guy. I can now understand why Madison sounded all shy and soft when she mentioned him. He's the type of man a girl could easily catch a crush on, if not more.

This is my impression of him before he speaks.

When he does speak? When he unfolds his tall, lithe body and takes command of the stage and thus the attention of everybody in the entire room? When his deep, rich, smooth voice rings out and puts me under its spell? It makes me go weak.

Oh, yeah, if I were even slightly inclined toward acting, I'd sign up for any class he was part of. I'd do just about anything he wanted so long as it meant being in his presence.

I don't think I've ever experienced this sort of deep, primal reaction to a man. Dr. Jake was probably the closest I've ever come to wanting to climb a man like he's a tree and clinging to him until I took my dying breath.

A dying breath brought about by mind-bending pleasure, of course.

One of the girls—somebody I haven't met yet—stands and joins him. They're a couple, clearly on the verge of breaking up. It's amazing actually, how much their body language tells me. They don't need to say out loud that they've been together for a long time and are dangerously close to the end of their relationship.

I see it in the way she tucks her hair behind her ears, the way her shoulders hunch up. The way he looks everywhere but at her when they're talking. The way he fidgets a little. The way she keeps tapping her foot and looking at the floor and closing in on herself. He tries to reach out, but she closes up even tighter than before.

It occurs to me that he cheated on her or otherwise broke her trust. How do I know this? I just do. I'm not even listening to their dialogue, but I know it. I'll have to ask about it later, after the performance.

This is a lot like writing a novel. Showing, not telling. It would be easy for either of them to come right out and vomit a bunch of backstories, and sure, that would be one way to make the audience understand what's playing out between these characters under the surface.

It's much more effective to convey this history through looks. Gestures. The things that aren't said are way more powerful than what is spoken.

When his arm shoots out and he cups the back of her head in one hand, pulling her in for a deep kiss, I'm not the only person in the audience who has to catch their breath in surprise.

She stiffens. I mean, the girl goes stiff as a board, and it's clear he's kissing her hard. Passionately. For all he's worth. But she's not having it. I almost want to tell him to stop.

The girl takes a step back once he lets her go.

Swipes the back of her hand across her mouth.

Wipes it on his shirt.

Walks away, leaving him alone.

He lowers his head, clenching his fists at his sides.

The lights go down, signaling the end of the scene.

"That was so powerful," the woman next to me whispers to the person on the other side. "No wonder she was excited to work with him on the scene."

I can't help myself. "What's the name of the actor?" I ask in a low voice.

She looks at me like I just landed on Earth this morning and haven't caught up on all the most important things. "Rafe Douglas. You've never seen him perform before?"

"I haven't. He's really good, huh?"

"He's going to be a star. No doubt." She then goes back to whispering with her friend while the actors performing the next scene get themselves ready.

I think I agree with that assessment. Rafe, or Rafael, or whatever he wants to be called is most definitely going to be a star someday.

And I absolutely have to meet him.

And if we end up making out, well, so be it. I'm sure I'll get through it.

Chapter Six

WE'VE BEEN AT this diner for twenty minutes, and I'm pretty sure half the group has been out for a cigarette twice since our arrival.

"I wouldn't have imagined there being so many smokers in the group."

Rafe grins from the other side of the long line of tables pushed together to accommodate us, and his blue eyes practically sparkle in the light reflecting off so much chrome trim. It's one of those old-school diners, very retro, right down to the little jukeboxes in the booths, where customers can play their favorite old songs.

"Can you imagine if smoking in public buildings were still legal?" he asks. "They'd be chain-smoking through the entire meal."

"Everybody must've been really stinky back in the day, huh?"

His grin widens. "I don't know if you're old enough to remember when the host at a restaurant would ask whether you wanted to sit in the smoking or nonsmoking section."

"I do! Gosh, I completely forgot about that. I

was pretty young back then." I sit back, looking him up and down. It's not exactly punishing, studying him this way. "You couldn't have been very old either."

"Not very. Definitely too young to smoke." He stretches his arms out over the backs of the chairs to his right and left.

Both of them are empty. Both were chosen by girls. They'd practically raced to get the chairs closest to him.

I can see why. And not only because he's physically one of the most beautiful, perfect specimens I've ever seen.

Because he's also charming. Genuine and warm and self-deprecating. Not an egomaniac. All points in his favor.

"So, did you go to school for acting?"

He nods slowly. "Carnegie Mellon."

"Wow. That's a great program there, isn't it?"

"I was lucky to get admitted."

He picks up his cup of coffee, which I notice he drinks black. I've never been someone who could manage that. The very thought makes my nose wrinkle a little.

"From what I saw tonight, it was more than luck. You're a very talented actor."

He offers a weak smile, glancing over one shoulder before leaning in toward me. "If you think that was something, you should see the other group I'm in. That's a secret. Only you're allowed to know."

Well, would you look at that? Sudden intimacy. The sense of sharing something only the two of us are in on.

Is he deliberately flirting? Or does he have no idea what it means when a gorgeous, talented man makes a girl feel special?

I'm going to go with the latter of the two. I might be giving him too much credit, but the few minutes we've spent chatting—along with the small talk we made after the performance—haven't given me the impression of him being a conceited jerk.

Though he's a good actor. I have to watch my opinions of him. I have a tendency to want to see the best in people, especially when the people in question are charming and have a mouth that practically begs to be kissed.

Bianca sits to his right when she comes in, Madison to his left.

Ashley sits at my left and nudges me with her elbow. "It's so neat, having you here."

"You're too sweet."

And she is. It's unusual, spending time with a fan like this. I guess there's something to be said for getting out in the world and talking to people, meeting them, finding out why they enjoy my work and what their lives are like and what reading romance does for them.

It's not easy, being an introvert. Even in college, I rarely got together with big groups of people like this. Sitting around a cluster of tables, stealing food off each other's plates, all that.

"You're like a big family," I note as I look up and down the length of the table.

There are ten people on either side and two squeezed in at both ends. It's easy to get caught up in the silliness and laughter and lightheartedness.

Rafe catches my eye and grins. "You're seeing us on a good night too."

Bianca notices the way my brows lift in curiosity. "He means, we're feeling good after the performances. We had an audience with great energy. Everything went well."

"So, if something had gone wrong, it would've been a different scene?" I mean, the heat was off the entire time, and I was sure an icicle would be hanging from the tip of my nose by the end. Is that considered normal?

"Honestly?" Rafe's grin widens into an ear-to-ear smile, and my gosh, it's like dawn breaking. I swear, the entire diner lights up from it. I feel myself opening up under its warmth, like a morning glory.

And I'm not the only one. If there were a means of measuring the amount of female adoration flowing his way …

Madison clears her throat before nudging Rafe. "Your pieces were incredible. Next time, I'd love to work on a scene with you. I think we could write something amazing."

"You're probably right." He nods, encouraging, and she just about melts into her chair.

I wonder if I'm the only one who notices, and I think I am. Everybody else is busy talking among themselves and their significant others. And since I'm new and not here with anyone it gives me the benefit of observing.

When our food arrives, I notice everyone has ordered, for the most part, fairly greasy stuff. Burgers, fries, breakfast platters—gotta love all-day breakfast—mozzarella sticks, potato skins. My mouth waters while I look at all of it.

I'd feel lame for ordering a crock of French onion soup if it wasn't for Rafe's salad.

He sees me eyeing it up and chuckles. "The last thing I need is something heavy in my stomach when I'm trying to sleep. I value sleep over just about everything else."

"Don't even bother trying to get him on the phone when he's asleep." Ashley giggles.

Am I the only one who sees how obvious it is that she's loving that little bit of intimacy? Like she knows something personal about him, like they have a special connection of some sort.

Or maybe I'm reading too much into it.

But I don't think I am. The thing about being an introverted writer is, I'm used to analyzing people without even consciously doing it. It's always been one of my party tricks—a trick only I know about. Reading body language, hearing what people say without saying a word.

Ashley has a crush on Rafe. So do Bianca and Madison and probably every woman at this table who likes men. Maybe a couple of the guys too. Who's to say? He's the star, the sun they revolve around.

And he has another group he's involved with. One the people at this table aren't supposed to know about. He doesn't want to hurt their feelings. He has a good heart, but he's not stupid. He's better than they are. There's training, and there's talent. And he has natural talent.

He knows he'll never go as far as he can if he doesn't expand his horizons and work with serious, committed actors. I have to give him credit for that; he could keep up this life of being a big fish in a small pond, could keep being idolized by less talented actors, but that won't get him anywhere.

"I guess you have to use your body a lot as an actor," I offer. "You want to make sure it's in good shape, so it'll do what you need it to do."

"You sound like him." Bianca rolls her eyes and nudges Rafe, who only shrugs before shoving a forkful of salad into his waiting mouth. It seems like she's not as enthused about her plate of fries, gravy, and cheese as she was before.

"That looks delicious," I sigh, eyeing her plate like I'm envious.

When she offers me a fry, I take it even though I don't particularly want one. At least she's smiling again.

"So, how did you all meet?" I ask, looking around. "I'm so interested in how you do things. I'm basically a hermit, so this is really neat."

Everybody looks at each other as the table falls into general silence. I see a lot of lifted shoulders, raised eyebrows.

"I don't remember," Madison admits. "It feels like we've always known each other."

"We sort of fell into each other's lives," Ashley explains. "One person had a friend who knew another person, and that person had a friend in the group ..."

"Got it. I sort of wish writers had something like what you have," I admit. I could use a writing family.

"You mean, there aren't groups for writers to get together and share their work?" Rafe looks and sounds skeptical. "There has to be, right?"

"Sure, I know at least three or four," Bianca adds, nodding to Rafe like the two of them are in on some secret.

"Huh." I have to sit back and think. "Yeah, I guess you're right. Though you're probably thinking more of playwriting, I would imagine."

"Probably, but there are all kinds of people writing things. Novelists, people writing memoirs, you name it." Rafe practically scowls at me. "You mean, you've never thought of that before?"

The girls look at me like I'm an object of pity. I

guess they feel bad about Rafe thinking I'm an idiot.

I don't feel bad. In fact, I'm a little annoyed. *Who does this guy think he is?*

"Four of my books made it to number one on the *New York Times* Best Sellers list, and all but one of my subsequent books have placed on the list. My next release is projected to hit the top spot on its debut." I fold my arms, arching an eyebrow. "I guess I've been too busy writing them to bounce ideas off other authors."

It's like the air has been sucked out of the room, and I know I made a mistake. A huge mistake. No way is this man going to want to get to know me after I not only snapped at him, but also pretty much rubbed my success in his face. Nobody likes a braggart.

Do they all think I am?

Ashley reacts first with an explosive laugh that draws the attention of people from surrounding tables. "Damn, son! She got you!"

Only when Rafe laughs with her does everyone else remember to breathe. Including me.

"Sorry," I mumble anyway since I still feel like it might've been more than a little jerky to mention my success.

He doesn't see it that way. "You're right though! You're totally right. You're on a completely different plane of existence from the rest of us."

"I did not mean it that way!" I insist. My cheeks are burning hotter than the still-piping soup in front of me.

"It's not a bad thing." His foot connects with mine under the table, nudging me a little. "Don't feel bad for being successful. Seriously. If anything, you give hope to the rest of us."

"You might be a writer while we're actors, but we're all artists. You managed to be successful, doing what you do." Bianca's eyes pretty much shine when she says it.

Madison looks the same way.

I don't have the heart to tell them I haven't exactly made it big. Yes, having a string of best sellers is a huge accomplishment, and I was lucky beyond measure to have it happen to me. Now that I've been on the other side of that improbable success, I realize now more than ever how precious it was. And how unusual since hardly anybody ends up with one best seller, much less four number-ones.

But I see now that they're sort of looking up to me, and as uncomfortable as it makes me, I don't have the heart to burst anybody's bubble.

"I should expand my horizons though," I remind her with a rueful grin. "Something I've been slowly but surely working on for almost a year now. Joining a group is the next logical step. Art can't be any good if it's stagnant, right?"

I never talk like this, but they're making me do it. It's their fault I'm becoming someone who talks about her art. Maybe I should start wearing a beret and refer to myself in the third person.

Writing is a form of art, but I care more about storytelling and creating worlds that immerse the reader into a place where they can forget their troubles for a little while. I have no illusions about my books being considered culturally significant or anything like that.

But these people are still dreaming that dream, and I won't let my jaded self get in the way.

He sees it too. He sees right through me. I can tell when he offers a slight smile before going back to his salad. Even though he's eating, his gaze keeps hitting me from beneath his lowered brow. Something tells me we're going to talk a lot more about this.

And I want to. I do. It's not an accident, the way the girls flock to him. The way no pair of eyes stays away from his part of the table for more than a few minutes at a time. The way conversations around us quiet down every time he speaks.

Yes, I want to talk with him. I'd like to do more than that, especially since my heart slightly flutters every time our eyes meet. For the sake of my new friends, I look away when we lock eyes. I don't want to upset them.

It's only when we're finishing up and saying *good-bye for now* that he edges a little closer to me. We're in front of the diner, and it's a bitter cold night.

"Maybe we should've gotten the good-byes out of the way inside," he murmurs, leaning down so his mouth is close to my ear. His breath forms a cloud between us. "It always takes a while."

I can't help but laugh softly. He's got such a kind way about him. A talent for making a girl feel like she's the only person in the entire world.

"I might lose my fingers in this cold."

He gasps before grinning. "Oh no. Then, how would you write those best sellers of yours?"

"Cute. I am sorry about that, by the way. Really. I didn't mean to brag or anything."

"You put me in my place. It's okay. I deserved it for being so incredulous. It's none of my business why you haven't joined a writing group. I don't know the first thing about how you work or why you do what you do."

"There's one way to change that."

I don't have time to tell him how we can change it before Bianca throws an arm around his shoulders. "Come on. Share our car with us?"

I take a step back to give them room. If he and Bianca have a thing going on, I won't get in the way. She seems like a sweet girl, and I'm not here to ruin anything.

Besides, I'm freaking freezing. My nose is starting to ache from it, not to mention the rest of my face.

Rafe's body goes stiff. For someone who's good at controlling his every move and muscle twitch when he's onstage, he doesn't cover his awkwardness well. "Thanks, but I was gonna stop off before going home. I'll walk."

"In this cold?" Bianca bites her lip.

"Come on!" Madison waves from the curb. "Our ride's here. I don't feel like being charged extra because the guy had to wait."

Bianca offers me a little wave before hurrying over to Madison, leaving Rafe and me alone-ish.

"Before we get interrupted again, can I take you to dinner sometime?" he asks all at once.

I answer right away, "Yes. I'd love that."

"I'll find you online. Isn't that how you found Ashley?" He winks, backing away. "See you soon, best-selling author."

"You're not gonna let me live that down, are you?"

His hair swings back and forth when he shakes his head hard, laughing, as I climb into the car waiting for me.

Am I craning my neck to catch one last look at him before pulling away? Maybe. Just maybe.

Chapter Seven

"AN ACTOR."

I manage to keep from rolling my eyes at my grandmother, but it's not easy. Not even a little. "What's wrong with that?"

"An actor."

"You said that already. And you make it sound like I told you he's a serial killer for kicks."

"He might be, for all you know."

I scoff.

"Well? You don't know this young man. And even if his future doesn't involve serial murder, can you justly say he has a solid career?"

"Do I have to run down the list of so-called solid family men who ended up being psycho killers?"

"No."

"You sure? Because I can think of several off the top of my head."

She wrinkles her nose. "Must you be morbid? One would think you wrote crime thrillers for a living."

"Writing isn't considered a solid career either. You know that, right?"

"Why must you downplay your success, my dear?" She reaches out to pat my cheek just a smidgen harder than she needs to. Still gentle, but just barely.

I can't help but notice how unsparkly she is today. Normally, I'm asking myself how she manages to lift her arms with so much hardware weighing her down. Diamonds are her usual favorite, and Lord knows she has enough of them to blind a person if the light hits her just right.

In fact, now that I'm paying attention, she looks downright ordinary. Still wearing a skirt, of course—I don't think I've ever seen her wear slacks, not once ever—and a silk blouse. Her hair is perfectly arranged, as always, in a sleek chignon.

Otherwise, there's nothing even remotely fabulous about her. Nothing the average passerby would notice outside of her beauty, which time hasn't managed to affect.

She notices me watching her because the woman doesn't miss a trick. "What is it? Do I have something on my face? Between my teeth?"

"No. You're okay."

"So, why are you looking at me the way you are?"

I shrug while lowering my teacup to the table in front of us. We're in the parlor today, which basically looks like it should be in a museum. Heck, it might as well be a museum, filled with priceless artwork that my grandmother and grandfather collected during their travels in the early days of their marriage. Before Mom was born, before they settled down into their roles as a married couple with a child.

"Honestly?" I wince a little when I ask since I know she's not going to want to hear what I have to say.

She tips her head to the side, fixing me with a hard stare from eyes that look a lot like mine. "Of course."

"You look and act more natural, more at home than I've ever seen you before."

She laughs at this, shaking her head. "Your writer's imagination is making you think that."

"I don't think so. You seem … at ease. Comfortable. Not so stiff and buttoned up." I sit up a little straighter, looking at her over the end of my nose. The way she typically looks at me, like a duchess passing silent judgment over her underlings.

And it earns me no favor.

"I hope you don't think you were imitating me by doing that."

"And if I am?" I lift my eyebrows because why the heck not? She's already annoyed with me. Might as well go all the way.

To my endless surprise, instead of scolding me, she cracks a tiny smile. "I don't appreciate being made fun of."

"We have that in common." I lean in, grinning. "I'm not trying to make fun. But don't tell me your relationship with Peter hasn't helped you lighten up a little bit."

She surprises me again by blushing. There's no disguising it, no hiding it. This is maybe the second time in my memory that she's shown a softer side. A more human side. I almost don't know how to act around her.

But that doesn't mean I can't have a little fun with this turn of events.

"Look at you," I whisper. "Blushing like a schoolgirl."

"Kathryn Antoinette." She can't even sound like she means it, not when she's so busy grinning like the Cheshire cat. "Don't make me regret having you over for tea."

"I would hope you wouldn't regret my visit." I sniff, trying to pretend to be insulted when, really, I'm happier than I've been in ages. For her sake, entirely for her sake.

She had been alone for too long. No matter how many times she'd sworn she didn't mind, that she could find male companionship whenever she was in the mood for it, I always harbored a sneaking suspicion there was a deep well of loneliness she didn't want me to see.

Peter comes in, carrying a tray of sandwiches and cookies. If the change in my grandmother is enough to make me happy, the change in her longtime butler and official beau might bring me to tears.

He seems younger, lighter on his feet, and he is even humming softly. Just looking at the two of them together reinforces my belief in the sort of things I've been writing about for years, the things I want so much to believe in. True love, devotion. The transformative power of being able to admit, after so long, that you love someone.

And the sweetness of being able to express that love. The freedom to indulge those feelings.

Peter couldn't allow himself to show the affection he'd developed for Grandmother over the decades as an employee. It's like this massive weight has been lifted from his shoulders.

Another difference: the fact that he sits down with us when, in the past, such a thing would have been unheard of. I mean, a servant? Sitting down with us to eat? The horror—for her anyway. Not for me.

Yet there he is, perched on the silk-covered sofa, sitting beside my grandmother.

I have to say, I'm impressed with my ability to play it cool in front of him, like this is nothing special or new. I feel like the slightest movement will pop their happy little bubble, and I don't want to do that. If it isn't weird for them, it's not weird for me.

"I hope you're making sure she obeys the doctor's orders," I tease.

Peter and I have always had a playful sort of relationship. I've told him for years that he is my favorite thing about her, and I meant it.

His eyes crinkle at the corners, but he manages to hide a smile. "Your grandmother understands the importance of obeying the doctor's orders. She knows she's far too important to too many people to treat this lightly. She was fortunate her heart attack was only mild. We wouldn't want to tempt fate and see what happens next time." He angles himself toward her. "Isn't that right?"

Meanwhile, I have to pretend to wipe my mouth with my napkin to hide my smile. For once, somebody's scolding my imperious grandmother even if he's being gentle about it.

She grumbles openly, though anybody who's known her as long as I have could see she likes the attention. She likes being cared for even if she doesn't always enjoy how that caring manifests itself.

"I know that's as good an answer as I'll get." Peter winks at me, and I swear, I could kiss him.

He is a godsend to her—to both of us really since, without him, I would spend my days worrying about her. I've never had to worry about her—and not only because she has a good head on her shoulders and more than enough money to make sure she's cared for until the end of her days, but also because I know she has somebody who loves her right by her side.

She lifts her delicate teacup with a sigh. "Once you decide to take a break from scolding me, you might spare a word or two for my granddaughter."

"Hey! Hold on a second. Don't try to turn this around on me."

"I'm doing no such thing."

"Yes, you are. Trying to change the subject, so Peter won't give you a hard time and probably tell me about all the times you've tried going against your cardiologist's orders."

Peter, meanwhile, laughs through this. "Why would I ever criticize Kathryn?"

"Thank you," I crow, throwing Grandmother a superior look. I manage to stop short of sticking my tongue out but only just barely.

"She's dating an actor. Can you imagine anyone less stable?"

"We're not dating, for one thing." I don't know why I feel the need to set the record straight, but I do. "We're going to dinner tomorrow night. That's not dating. That's a single date."

"This is for your next book, I imagine?"

I nod, and he offers a shrug.

"I don't see anything so wrong with that. Kathryn knows what's best for her. She always has. It must run in the family."

Oh, he's good. He is very good. Sometimes, I forget he's known her longer than I have. He knows exactly what to say to butter her up. When she's not looking, I give him a thumbs-up. To his credit, he manages only a quick little smile, which is gone by the time she turns back to him.

"It's only that I wish she would become serious about someone. Someone substantial. Someone who will take care of her."

My shoulders slightly sag before I sit upright again. "I don't need anyone to take care of me. We've had this discussion before."

"I don't mean financially."

"Neither do I."

Peter, smooth as ever, steps in before my temper flares. "I think what your grandmother is referring to is having someone to look after you. Eventually, everyone needs looking after. Someone to be there for you in troubled times."

"And if I decide to settle down, what does him being an actor have to do with it? An actor could be by my side during troubled times just as well as a doctor could."

Clearly, we all know who she's talking about. She still wishes I hadn't ended things with Jake Becker, but that's easy for her to say. It wasn't her relationship.

"I never said you had to settle down with a doctor," she snaps.

Peter chuckles, glancing her way. "No, but you wouldn't be upset if she did."

"Would you mind telling me whose side you're on?" she asks with a teasing note in her voice.

They share a look that goes a long way toward melting the ice that started forming around my heart, thanks to this turn in conversation.

Honestly, they're the cutest thing in the entire world.

I'm not an idiot. I know where her concern is coming from. Not only from a caring grandmother, but also from somebody who's found love again. People who are in the honeymoon phase of their relationship want everybody to feel the same way they do. She has Peter, and Peter has her. She wants me to have the same happy security.

And it's not like I wouldn't enjoy it.

Just that I haven't found it.

Chapter Eight

WHY AM I so nervous?

It's not like I've never been on a date before. I probably haven't been on half as many dates as people would expect a romance author to go on, but still they've increased substantially within the last few months.

So, why is my hand shaking as I apply my mascara? If I'm not careful, I'll end up poking my eye out. Not the most attractive look, though I guess I could make up for it with a sparkly eyepatch or something like that. Unfortunately, I'm already running late, and I'm confident there isn't an eyepatch store on the way to my date.

By the time I'm finished getting ready, wearing more makeup than I have in recent memory, I barely have time to run downstairs and hop in the car that my phone just told me was waiting by the curb.

Did I remember to put on deodorant? Crap, I can't remember if I put on deodorant. As soon as I know the driver isn't looking, I take a quick sniff test.

I smell fine, but I'm sweating. A lot.

Jeez, I wasn't this worked up before seeing my adolescent superstar crush playing live and in person. That's saying something because I was pretty much on the verge of an emotional explosion all night long. Like a powder keg waiting for the spark to set me off.

Maybe it's because I genuinely like Rafe. He seems like a decent person. And while I've created a rough sketch of how I want my new book to go, I do need his help. I need to know about actors. How they think, their process. That's what it's called, right?

It wouldn't hurt if things heated up a little bit between us either. I mean, I'm supposed to be writing hot romance, aren't I? Goodness knows I've been on the verge many times, but it would be nice to finish my sexy scenes from experience instead of inspiration. Maggie keeps asking for more, and honestly, I'd love to be able to give it to her.

But only if he's single and completely unattached. I don't want to step on any toes. Ever since he reached out to me the day after we met to make arrangements—yes, the day after—I've been wondering about the girls. Ashley and the others. All of them seemed highly protective of him, which leads me to wonder if there's more than unrequited crushing going on.

Even though I remind myself time and again to keep my expectations low and play this as cool as possible, there's no holding back the nervous thrill that runs through me when I see Rafe waiting for me outside the cute little restaurant with twinkle lights outlining the window and strung up in the trees out front.

Gosh, he looks good, but then I'm sure he'd look good in just about anything. He wore a black sweater and pants for the workshop—everybody wore black; I guess that was decided upon in advance. Tonight, I'm treated to a nice pair of jeans and a gray turtleneck under a peacoat, the collar raised against the January air.

In a word, *yum*.

He smiles when I get out of the car, a genuine sort of smile that crinkles his eyes at the corners. "I was afraid you wouldn't show," he admits with a sheepish little laugh.

I'm half-tempted to ask if he hit his head recently because who in their right mind wouldn't show up?

"Why would you think that?"

"I don't know. You've got your life together, and I …"

"Come on, Rafe." I nudge him a little with my elbow. "An actor of all people should know about the power of illusion. Trust me, I don't have it all together. And I'd have been ten kinds of stupid to stand you up."

It's not until we're inside, taking our seats in the dimly lit restaurant—it's nice, charming, with strings of even more white lights crisscrossing the ceiling and draped along the walls—that I have a chance to admire the way his turtleneck hugs his chest and arms. He's not quite as lean as I thought he was in the slightly baggier sweater he wore before. He really does take care of himself.

I, for one, am grateful.

"This place is so cute!" I can't stop admiring the tiny, twinkling lights, how they warm the place up and give it a sense of magic. "I don't come down to the Village much, but whenever I do, I end up wishing I spent more time here."

"Where do you spend your time?"

Terrific. This is really going to make me sound exciting.

"In my apartment, honestly. That's where I spend most of my time. It's sort of a habit I've developed, for better or worse."

"Where is your apartment?"

"On the West Side," I say shyly, hoping I don't sound like I'm bragging again.

One corner of his mouth twitches, pulling upward just a bit. He skewers me with those eyes of his. "Where on the West Side? I have lots of friends who live there."

Why does my skin feel so itchy all of a sudden? Like I want to crawl right out of it. "Uh, near the park."

"So, Upper. Upper West Side." He laughs in time with the flushing of my cheeks. "Don't be embarrassed! It's just your address. I was genuinely curious. Hell, if I could afford an apartment on the

Upper West Side, I probably wouldn't leave either."

"It helps that I have a job I can do from home."

"No doubt. Good for you. Please," he adds, reaching across the table and closing his fingers over mine. The suddenness of his touch takes my breath away. "Don't think I hold it against you. I don't. Sure, we had that little dustup at the diner, but it didn't mean anything. If I didn't think you were quality, I wouldn't have bothered to ask you to dinner."

I can buy that. Then again, with him looking at me the way he is and his thumb stroking my knuckles, I'm in a position to buy pretty much anything he's selling.

"I'm sorry. I don't know why I feel so uneasy. It's so weird, spending time with a fan like Ashley. I'm always afraid I'll end up disappointing someone."

He offers one quick, soothing squeeze to my hand before withdrawing his. I wish he hadn't, but eating with only one hand would be sort of awkward.

"Why do you think that? I can't imagine you disappointing anybody."

"You said it yourself though. You made a comment outside about me having my life together. People expect certain things from you when you've written something and they've read it. They expect you to be … something special. Different from them, even better than them, even though we all have talents of our own. And here I am, just a normal person. Somebody who barely leaves the apartment because I'm always working on one project or another, who barely has time to go shopping so I order all of my clothes online. The delivery people working in my neighborhood know me by my first name."

"You know what I think it is?" He props his chin up on one hand, still looking me straight in the eye. It should be unnerving, but it isn't—and not only because I want to drown in those eyes of his. They're so intense. "I think we put people on a pedestal to keep them separated from us because if we admit to ourselves that they're only regular people like us, it would mean having to turn inward to figure out why we haven't reached that level when they could do it. Do you know what I mean?"

Jeez, he's smart.

"So, for instance, let's say I happen to have a huge, disgusting crush on a famous movie star."

He snickers softly but manages to keep a straight face for the most part. "Right."

"It's easier for me to think of them as being something special because, otherwise, I might have to ask myself why I haven't achieved everything I'm capable of if they were able to achieve it for themselves."

"Exactly. Everyone needs somebody to look up to, even to aspire to. I guess, when you think of it that way, the world would be a pretty bleak place if we didn't have anybody to base our dreams on."

That's something to ponder in the back of my mind as we order. Thanks to my overprepared best friend rubbing off on me over the years, I did a little advance research on the restaurant when Rafe suggested it and learned they served a delicious risotto, so I order that along with a glass of chardonnay.

"And I'll have the grilled salmon with a double order of greens," he decides, flashing our server a killer smile that leaves her giggling softly as she takes the menus.

It's not the first time I've been on a date with a man capable of reducing grown women to giggling little girls, and I can't say it's not the tiniest bit gratifying.

Hey, I'm only human.

"Do you get that a lot?" I ask in a whisper.

He offers a blank stare. "Get what?"

"You know what I mean." I bat my eyelashes and make kissing noises with pursed lips.

He covers his mouth with the back of one hand to stifle a laugh. "Come off it."

"Are you serious? Or is this false modesty? Because if it's false modesty, I'm not impressed."

"I have a lot of faults, but false modesty isn't one of them."

"So, you honestly don't notice women falling over you?"

This is supposed to be a joke, but it's clear he

doesn't see it that way. Worry lines appear between his brows, and his mouth tips downward into a frown.

Instantly, I regret ever saying it. "I'm sorry. I was only joking."

"Oh, I know. It's just that you made me think of the other night. It can be sort of embarrassing, to be honest with you."

"What can?"

"Always feeling like somebody wants something from me. I don't want to name any names since I'm not that guy, but there's only so much I can handle gracefully. I don't like being hung on. I don't like people hovering around me."

I know exactly what he means, but I have to give him credit for being polite about it. He's trying to be a gentleman, but I can see through his veiled language. That, and I remember how he stiffened up when Bianca threw an arm around him.

"I think now is as good a time as any to ask you if you're involved with anybody in the group. I don't want anyone getting upset that we're out together like this."

He shakes his head, and my heart practically sings. Ashley is a nice girl, and I would like to get to know her better, but I wouldn't want to cause friction.

"No. I mean, in the past, I hooked up with a couple of the girls. I won't lie. We've all been together for a few years with other people sort of floating in and out at different times. It was a long time ago, but I guess there's a reason they say men and women can't be friends after they've crossed the line."

"It did seem like at least one of them was into you." Many more than one, but I'm trying to be tactful.

"I hate to say it, but that's just one more reason I've been spending a lot more time with the other group I mentioned. Don't get me wrong. I knew what I was getting into when I hooked up with the girls. I'm not a child, and I'm not going to lie. But it's uncomfortable, especially when they get all touchy, like they own me. This other new group, they're committed to their craft. There's no personal stuff among us to get in the way of the work. I've learned and grown so much in my time with them." He practically glows when he talks about them. His voice takes on the sort of reverent tone I'd expect to hear from a religious devotee.

"I hate to ask, but why do you hang around with the original group then?"

He averts his gaze and shifts a little in his chair as our server brings our drinks. I notice the way she tries to catch his eye, but he's too busy examining the tablecloth, looking uncomfortable.

Meanwhile, she won't look at me, and I sort of wish she would. I mean, he's here with me. Why is she making puppy dog eyes at him?

"Thank you," I chirp, and that seems to be

enough to move her feet.

He chuckles softly, still lost in thought. "To answer your question, I feel bad. I don't want to leave them. I don't want them to think I think I'm something special."

I can't help it. "But you are something special."

"You're just saying that. Ashley told me you were writing a book about actors, and I know you're here tonight for research. You don't have to stroke my ego. I would've come out with you either way."

"Do I give off the vibe of somebody who uses people? Because you're starting to make me feel bad." His eyes fly open wide, but I don't give him a chance to respond before continuing, "I've been looking forward to tonight ever since you sent me that message. And not because of a book."

"For real?"

"For real. I'm not the actor here, and I'm a terrible liar. Ask anybody."

"That's good to know since I would've been pretty bummed out at the thought that you weren't interested in anything else but your work."

I'm glad I'm wearing long sleeves or else he would be able to see the goose bumps all over my arms. How can I help it? I'm not made of stone, and he's doing things to me with those eyes of his. It's like I'm being hypnotized.

And I don't have a problem with it. In fact, I like it.

I like it so much that I decide before our entrées have even shown up that I'm going to invite him back to my Upper West Side apartment once we've finished eating.

And not for research.

Then again, maybe it will turn out to be research.

Maggie wants me to spice things up after all.

Chapter Nine

"So, THIS IS how the other half lives." Rafe lets out a low whistle when he steps into the apartment, sliding his hands into his pockets and nodding slowly as he takes in the view from the front windows. "Not bad. Not bad at all."

"Where do you live? You never did tell me."

As I'm closing the door, I take a quick look out into the hall and listen for the sound of Matt on the other side of his door. His apartment seems quiet. Maybe he's out for the night.

Good. I don't need him blasting horror-movie sound effects this time around. I still haven't gotten over that, especially since his timing couldn't have been worse. It was bad enough for a man to whisper another woman's name in my ear while in bed with me. The ear-piercing shrieks that immediately followed made me want to scream along with them.

Rafe shrugs out of his coat, handing it to me so I can hang it up. "I have a studio in Alphabet City. It's really just a room somebody somehow found a way to add a small bathroom to. It would make a good-sized bedroom for some little kid."

I know I shouldn't feel embarrassed. Still, I can't help it. I have so much space, and I'm only one person.

"Alone, I hope?"

He throws his head back and laughs at this. "God, yes. I can barely turn around without bumping into something as it is."

"Can I get you something to drink?"

He asks for water, so I bring him a bottle along with a glass of wine for myself, and we sit together on the sofa.

Once we settle in, I ask, "What about room-mates? You could afford something a little bigger if you lived with somebody else."

"True, but there would probably be the same amount of living space. Twice the apartment, twice the people. Know what I mean?" He waves a dismissive hand before opening his water. "I don't have it that bad. I know plenty of people who live in literal dumps, apartments the size of closets. I have a room, a tiny stove, a tiny refrigerator, and a tiny sink to go with my very tiny bathroom. I have my books, a TV, a bed."

"There's something to be said for only using as much as you need, I guess."

"Honestly, that's something that means a lot to me." He angles his body toward me while mine is angled toward him, so we're sitting close enough that our knees touch. "We live in such a materialistic world, don't we? Don't get me wrong; this apartment is beautiful. But I've never needed much. My parents were sort of hippies, and a lot of their beliefs rubbed off on me."

"My mom was kinda like that too."

His head snaps back a little, like he's surprised.

"I grew up in a little apartment in Brooklyn. My grandparents were very wealthy—my grandmother still is, I should say—but Mom didn't want to live that life. And she didn't want to raise me the way she had been raised. We were just normal people."

"How did you end up here then? What does she think about your fantastic view?"

It's not his fault. People of our general age don't immediately assume somebody's parents are already dead.

"She's not with us anymore. Neither is my dad." I look down at my wine, swirling it in the glass.

He touches my knee, and when I pry my eyes from my wine, I find him looking dismayed. "I'm so sorry. I shouldn't have assumed."

"It's okay. It's been a long time now. And, yes, maybe my grandmother did have some influence over the apartment I chose, but it was sort of a celebratory lease signing. I had just graduated college and sold my latest book. I was on top of the world."

"All things considered, you could have done a lot worse than leasing a gorgeous apartment. Especially at that age! I'd say you have a good head on your shoulders." He winks.

"I like to think so." I wink right back.

"I'm guessing you live alone."

"Yeah, not a roommate in sight. Do you ever get lonely?" I don't know where that question came from. It fell right out of my mouth before I had the time to critique it.

He doesn't seem to think it's a weird question though—at least, he doesn't skip a beat before shaking his head. "If anything, I wouldn't be a very good roommate."

"How come?"

"I keep terrible hours. I tend bar at Oscar's—ironic, right? That's how I make ends meet."

"I can't believe I never thought to ask you that."

Clearly, he doesn't make enough money from working with these little theater groups to live in Manhattan.

"It's decent money. So, I pretty much sleep during the day and work at night. I usually get home around five in the morning, if I don't stop out to get something to eat with some of the cooks. When I'm not sleeping or working, I'm getting what exercise I can in a small space."

"I like to do yoga here. What do you do?"

Whatever it is, it's working for him.

"The basic stuff. Push-ups, crunches, lunges, and squats. I have a set of free weights. I also do a lot of stretching and breathing exercises. Breath control is hugely important."

"I wouldn't have thought of that." I can't help but snicker, thinking back on our time at the diner. "It seems like a lot of your friends don't feel the same way about breath control, smoking the way they do."

He looks sort of stern, and now, I wonder if that was the right thing to say. I hope he doesn't think I was insulting his friends.

As it turns out, that isn't the case.

"You want my honest opinion?"

"Sure."

"That's just one of the reasons they'll never go as far as they want to go."

My eyes widen.

"I'm serious," he insists. "If you treat your craft like it's nothing more than a hobby, how can you expect to find any lasting success? Or any success at all? When I was in college, it became so clear. We were doing a big show, and all of us were hoping to be nominated for the American College Theater Festival. Judges would come in to evaluate our performances, that sort of thing. Everybody wanted to have a chance to compete at the national level. Anyway, only about half of the cast took it seriously. They quit drinking and smoking, stopped staying up late and eating junk, and basically worked their asses off. The other half did like they always had. Which half do you think got sent on to the festival?"

"And let me guess. You were one of the people

who got nominated."

He lifts a shoulder, offering a faint smile. "It was obvious which of us took the production seriously and which ones didn't. Even a bunch of judges, who had never met any of us before that one night, saw it. It makes a difference."

He leans in, and intensity practically leaks from his pores. His voice deepens as he says, "For me, acting isn't a hobby or a dream. It's what I do. This is my craft. It's not my sole purpose in life, but it's a big part of it. And if I'm ever going to make a name for myself or even earn a living at it, I have to dedicate myself to being as good as I can be."

There go the goose bumps again.

"I have to admit, you're a little bit overwhelming." When his face falls, I add, "In a good way! Really. I don't think I've ever met anyone as devoted as you. And for what it's worth, it was obvious to me, watching the performances the other night, that you have much greater dedication to your work. This isn't a game for you."

He relaxes against the cushions, grinning like I just said the magic words he'd been waiting to hear. "You saw that? You're not just saying it?"

"Not at all. It seemed like—and I'm sorry if I'm crossing the line by saying this—the rest of the group sat around at the diner, throwing these names around. I even recognized some of them. Strasberg and the method acting versus other approaches. And sure, it sounded interesting. But those are just words unless you back it up with action."

His mouth falls open before his eyes light up. "How is it you see everything so astutely? I mean, it's like you're reading my mind. You're saying things I've thought for such a long time."

"It's always easy for an outsider to step in and observe and draw conclusions," I offer with a shrug.

"No, no." He touches my knee again, and this time, his hand stays put. "No, it's more than that. You have insight and intelligence. I guess they come in handy when you're writing about people. Especially relationships."

"So, you don't think it's corny?" I tease, though there's more than a little bit of truth to my teasing. "Being a romance writer, I mean. You don't think I'm a loser for writing porn?"

"You don't write porn though. Hell, even if you did, who cares? You do it well enough that readers love it and want more of it. But last time I checked, the *Times* doesn't have a list of the best-selling porn—unless I'm missing something." A wicked grin follows this, and a twinkle is in his eye. "Hell, I might have to subscribe if that's the case."

I give him a playful nudge that's really nothing more than an excuse to touch him. Good Lord, his body is miraculous. So tight and firm, but not showy or obnoxious. "So, it's not corny? What I do?"

"Not at all. Listen, you might get that treatment from some people but not from me. I have nothing but respect for the amount of work you must put into what you do. I mean that."

"Really?"

"I know how hard it is to create what looks like a realistic relationship onstage or in a play I'm writing. I can't imagine what it would be like to write a whole book about it and actually have people want to read it. Much less more than one book."

It's like I've been holding my breath for years, and I finally have the opportunity to let it go. Somebody gets it. Hayley gets it, and my grandmother doesn't have a problem with me writing romance. I'm sure that, somewhere inside her, she'd rather I was somebody's well-groomed wife, carrying a Birkin bag on one arm and a baby in the other, though she wouldn't say it out loud.

But I've never felt like the rest of the people in my life take me seriously. Even Matt makes his jokes, though he pretty much laughs about everything I do.

This guy gets it. He gets how hard it can be sometimes. That my work is more than throwing a few sex scenes onto the page, strung together by a thin plot. I try to tell stories based on emotion, compelling enough that readers want to keep turning the page.

All of this bubbles up in me as I place my wineglass on the coffee table. He follows my lead and leaves his water there before taking my face between his hands and pulling me in for a passionate kiss.

He takes his time, his thumbs stroking my cheeks while his tongue glides along my lips. I part them to let him in, and he groans softly when I wrap my arms around his shoulders and press everything I can against him—chest, torso, legs.

It's been a while. What can I say? I'm a little eager, and I've been lusting after him ever since the second I saw him onstage.

So, when he lowers me to the sofa, I go willingly.

When he stretches himself out on top of me, our bodies touching from head to toe, I wrap one leg around his and pull him closer, making him groan louder this time and plunge his tongue deeper into my mouth while he moves his hips against my thigh.

When he growls faintly and pulls back, looking down at me with half-closed eyes and his mouth parted so he can breathe in short, heavy bursts, I try to pull him back down for more. So much more. My body is singing, my heart racing, blood rushing.

Yet there's regret when his eyes open fully. "If we keep going like this," he pants, his face still close to mine, "I don't think I'll want to stop."

"What's so bad about that?"

And who the heck is speaking through my

mouth? That is so not like me. Not even a little bit. I'm usually the one second-guessing everything, overthinking to the point of forgetting why I started thinking in the first place.

He pushes himself up onto his elbows, one on either side of me, and flashes a rueful grin. "I'm trying to learn my lesson. Remember earlier, when we talked about me hooking up with those other girls? Don't get me wrong; I don't think of you as just being one of them. But I don't want to make that mistake again either. Doing whatever I want without thinking of the consequences."

This is so not the time for him to be experiencing a crisis of conscience.

"I understand that," I murmur with a sinking heart while the rest of me wonders what about me isn't enough to make him want to throw his principles out the window for a little while.

I'm sure that if it wasn't for the general throbbing ache all over my body, I'd understand where he was coming from. I might even respect him for holding back.

But again, I'm aching over here.

He tucks a strand of hair behind my ear. "You're beautiful. So beautiful. I wanna take my time with you, if that's okay. I want to know so much more about you before we come together that way. I don't want this to be just another hook-up, if you get what I mean. Does that sound stupid?"

"Not at all."

He snickers quietly, planting a kiss on my nose and then on both cheeks. "It doesn't sound like you mean it."

"I do mean it. I'm just ... well, to be honest, you make a girl feel things."

He thrusts his hips, pushing himself against my thigh with a tight groan. "You make me feel things, too, and I'm sure I'm gonna have blue balls the rest of the night. I just want to avoid making the same mistakes over and over. I'm sorry."

"Nothing to apologize for. I mean it." I give him one more kiss before sliding out from under him while he works his way to a sitting position.

"I'd better go anyway," he decides, checking his phone. "I promised I'd call my scene partner. We're working on a piece we're presenting this weekend to the rest of the group and, you know, a few guests. Would you be interested in coming?"

"Sure, I'd love to." And not only for the sake of my book. Watching him in action is something else, like witnessing something special being born. The opening of a flower. The birth of a star. "And I guess I'd better get some work done. I always work better at night."

"Another night owl." He kisses me once more at the door after putting on his coat. He's warm and tender but strong, too, and still slightly demanding. Reminding me of the passion we came close to sparking into life back there on the sofa. "It seems like we have a lot in common, Miss Valentine."

Yes, and enough chemistry to make my toes curl before either of us has taken off a stitch of clothing.

Something tells me I'm going to enjoy writing this book.

Chapter Ten

I'LL SAY THIS for Rafe: he knows how to light a fire under a girl—and I'm not talking about her sexy parts.

Well, her sexy parts too. But that isn't what I'm referring to right now.

Right now, I'm referring to the fact that, as soon as I woke up these last few mornings, I've been raring to go. I want to find other writers to bounce ideas off of. I want to meet up with them and learn about their approach to writing. Maybe there's something I don't know. Maybe there's something that might work for me. I only need to learn from others.

Which is what has me looking around online for local writing groups. Not to sound snobby or anything, but I'm not looking for amateurs. I want to find people who've already been published or who at least have agents on their team. People who are serious about their writing, who have a career path in mind.

Unfortunately, as I scroll through one description after another, it seems like that's all I can find.

People who write short stories or who need feedback on an excerpt or single chapter.

Which is fine for people who don't already have a career. But not so fine for me.

I decide to pare down my search by adding the word professional to the keywords. Hopefully, that will narrow things down and keep me from wasting too much time.

Bingo.

I lean closer to the screen to read more. There's a group that meets up weekly in a coffee shop on the other side of the park to talk about their latest projects and to compare notes. Twice a month, an industry professional pays a visit—agents, editors, publicists—and they answer questions or give a presentation on changing trends. This sounds perfect for me.

It looks like they meet on Wednesdays, which works. Then again, just about any day of the week works for me. It's worth a try, so I shoot a message to the group's admin to ask if I can stop over and sit in on a meeting. I'm not trying to invade their space. Plus, my introverted self won't let me barge right on in without making sure I'm welcome.

Okay, so that's done. I can actually say I tried. And if I never hear back from them, I can always try again.

Maybe it's the conversation with Rafe the other night—all this talk about craft and honing it and being as good as he can be—but it now seems silly that I've never done this before. How thoughtless of me. Maybe a little prideful too. I mean, having my first book purchased and published right out of the gate is hardly anything to complain about, but it sort of helped me skip the steps most writers go through. Getting to know other writers, critiquing their work, having my work critiqued.

Nobody wants to have their work critiqued, but it's something we all have to go through.

With that in mind, I go back to what I started writing after Rafe left the apartment. I was horny as all get-out, putting it mildly, so I launched straight into a scene reminiscent of what had just taken place.

Ryder slid his hand over Fiona's jean-clad thigh, an inch at a time, and her skin practically sizzled, even with a layer of denim between her aching flesh and his skillful fingers. More. She wanted more. She needed more.

Watching him onstage was one thing, but having him between her thighs was something miraculous. This man—the one so many women in the audience had sighed over when he performed—he was hers for now, only hers.

And he was doing things to her that nobody had done in a long time. Waking up parts of her that had been asleep for ages, to the point where she couldn't remember just when they had been awake in the first place.

"Do you like it when I touch you?" he breathed between kisses, his breath hot against her already-heated skin. "Tell me how much you like it."

If she hadn't already been flushed all over, she definitely would have reddened at this request. "I like it," she whispered, straining upward so their mouths could meet again.

He pulled back, teasing. "You can do better than that," he whispered.

She groaned, frustrated, every inch of her body desperate for more of what they'd only started to explore together. "It feels good. I want more."

"Where does it feel good?" His hand started to slide upward again, and she closed her eyes as fresh waves of pleasure radiated from that point of contact. "Here, in this moment. Feel your body. Experience it. Breathe deep, be present."

She hadn't signed up for an acting lesson, had she? Something told her if she didn't do what he said, he would take his hand away along with the rest of him, and she would just die if he did that. She needed him too badly, with all her body. "It feels so good where you touch me."

"Good. But how does it feel? Tell me more."

His fingers pressed harder, digging into her flesh, and she bit down on her lip to hold back a whimper. This was torture, the most exquisite torture.

"It's like, wherever you touch me, I feel it deep inside. And I want more. Like my skin is on fire and I want it to keep burning."

He rewarded her by allowing his hand to slide over the curve of her ass, and she thought she might die from the excruciating, sweet ache between her legs. When she cried out, her head falling back, he lowered his head to taste the skin of her neck.

Okay, so my imagination ran away with me a little. I would like to think that if we had gone further, it would have been like this. No, Rafe would not turn our playtime into an acting lesson—at least, I sure hope he wouldn't.

Something chimes on my computer, making me jump. I have so many stinking tabs open; it's hard to keep track of which one the sound came from. Thankfully, one of the tabs in my browser is blinking, indicating the site.

The writing group? Did somebody get back to me this quickly?

No, as it turns out, it's a message from Ashley. I'm smiling when I open it.

Sadly, my smile dies soon after.

Did you go out with Rafe? Just the two of you?

The hostility comes at me in waves. The girl doesn't even need to be in front of me for me to feel what's behind her question. My knee-jerk reaction is to ask how she even knows we were out together, but I'll let that go for now. There's no reason to be secretive or defensive.

Yes, I did. He gave me a lot of insight for my next book. Acting is sort of like writing, I guess. People don't give nearly enough credit to actors for all the work they put into their craft.

Are you sure that's it?

Okay, now, my irritation is starting to bubble up. There are several directions in which I could take this, most of which would end up with us fighting. Granted, I don't know this girl, but that doesn't mean I want to fight. Besides, sad but true, there's something to be said for not earning myself a reputation with fans. All I need is for her to start spreading stories about me being nasty.

I'm not sure I understand what you're asking, I reply. *Is there something I should know? Did I step on toes? I didn't mean to.*

It takes a while for her to submit a response. All I can tell from the little ellipsis that keeps popping in and out of the chat window is that she is trying to formulate a response but keeps going back and forth with what to say. Finally, a lengthy message comes back.

It's just that you should know he's sort of a man-whore. He's pretty much stuck it in most of the girls in our group and some of their roommates. I don't want to see you get hurt by him. You don't know him very well, so you don't know how he is.

I lean back in my chair, reading it again and again. Are we in college or something? Or even worse, high school? I sure hope the writing group isn't like this because I don't think I could handle that level of drama.

I think you have the wrong idea, I reply. *Rafe reached out to me and asked if I would like to go to dinner and, I accepted. We talked a lot about acting and what it takes to craft a solid performance. Anything beyond that is between Rafe and myself. I appreciate your concern. I really do.*

I mean, what else am I going to say? I knew

there would end up being some sort of drama, didn't I? Which is why I made a point to ask whether he was involved with anybody from that group of actors. Not only do I not want to hurt anybody's feelings, but again, I also can't afford to create an image where I'm swooping in and stealing men from other women.

Just watch your back with him, she warns. *You seem like a nice person, and nobody wants to see you get hurt.*

I hate to say it, but it's like she thinks I was born yesterday. Like I can't see through this concern of hers. She has a crush on him and doesn't want me to get in the way of that. If I knew her better, I'd even say that. I might ask if she had feelings for him and apologize if I came off as a threat of some sort.

Thank you for looking out for me, I decide to reply.

Honestly, this is why I spend so much time by myself. It's so hard to navigate situations like this, to make sure everybody's happy and nobody gets hurt. Not to sound like I'm sitting too high on my horse, but facts are facts: when I'm all up in my feelings and trying to deal with drama like this, it takes away from my ability to work.

So, are you going to go out with him again?

I have to get up and walk around the room, shaking out my hands. It would be so easy to tell her to mind her own business, and that's exactly what I want to do. Because it's my business, not hers. If I decide to hump Rafe half to death in the middle of Central Park, that's what I'll do.

One thing is for sure: I can't tell her the truth. I'm going to his group with the more professional actors over the weekend. He already texted me the information, and I'm looking forward to it. But she's not supposed to know about that, and it isn't my business to spill the beans.

I don't mean any offense, I type, standing in front of the laptop, *but that's between Rafe and me. Please, don't take that the wrong way. I'm not trying to ruin anybody's life or anything. But I didn't know he was off-limits for dinner or a drink. If there's something I don't know, please tell me. I don't want to hurt anybody.*

She comes back right away this time. *I'm just warning you. He's been around. Don't fall for his lines. You seem like a nice person, and it would be a shame if he got under your skin like he does with everybody else.*

At least I can openly roll my eyes without her seeing. *Thank you for reaching out. I appreciate it. And I would love to hang out sometime if you're free. Let me know, and we can meet up someplace, okay?*

I don't get a response to that.

What did she expect me to say? Did she want me to pretend like I had never seen Rafe and never would again?

"See?" I ask my otherwise empty apartment. "This is why I keep to myself."

I then pick up the phone to send a quick message to Rafe, the subject of all this drama. *Are you free tonight? Nothing important or time-consuming, but I wanted to tell you about a conversation I just had.*

It's not until after I send the text that I remember

his normal schedule. He doesn't usually get up early in the day. Neither do I, but I did this morning. I felt so bright-eyed and bushy-tailed.

A few hours pass before he gets back to me.

I'm working tonight, but it would be nice if you stopped in. I always have time to chat. Is everything okay?

I can't help but smile, knowing he wants to see me, that he would take time out of what's sure to be a busy night.

Everything's fine, really. I just want to bounce something off you.

Because honestly, I can't take much more of this nonsense. I didn't sign on for the entire group to monitor my every move.

And I hate to tell them, but if I have my way, things between Rafe and me are going to heat up. I don't want to make his life any more complicated either. He deserves to know what might be waiting on the horizon.

Chapter Eleven

OKAY, I HAVE no idea what he was talking about when he said there would be time for us to chat.

It's Thursday night, which everybody knows became the new Friday a long time ago. And Friday is now Saturday, though I don't know what that makes Saturday. Sunday? Saturday Part Two? Either way, the place is hopping, and I'm nearly swallowed up by the crowd around the bar when I try to get anywhere close enough for Rafe to notice me.

I wish I had thought to ask Hayley to join me, but she's too busy anyway. I just know that if she were here, she would get these people out of the way without so much as an apology. Then again, she tends to part a crowd without trying. She has that way about her.

But no, it's just little old me, getting jostled back and forth as people try to elbow their way closer to the bar.

Good thing I'm not in any hurry.

What's also good is the eye candy working behind the bar. There are three bartenders in all, which still hardly seems to be enough to handle the absolutely insane amount of people in this place. The other two are girls, dressed in tight shirts cut low enough to leave nothing to the imagination, but it's Rafe who captures my attention and holds it.

He moves with an effortless sort of grace—gliding back and forth, quick and efficient—but he's also devastatingly charming as he fixes drinks and makes small talk with the customers. His smile is warm, friendly, without so much as a hint of fatigue or strain. Frankly, I don't know how he does it because if I had a hundred people demanding something from me all at once, my head would explode.

It takes me around ten minutes of watching him before I can finally get close enough for him to see me.

"There you are!" he calls out, and his smile widens from ear to ear.

The man is magic, I swear, because that alone is enough to light me up inside. He's truly happy to see me.

"I managed to keep from being trampled!" I call out, and a few people nearby hear me and laugh in understanding.

"I think you've earned yourself a drink. What will it be?"

"A dirty martini," I decide. "Vodka. Extra olives."

"What did you want to talk about?" he asks as

he pours, though there isn't time for me to tell him before one of the other bartenders slides up behind him and gestures to a customer at the other end of the bar. He shoots me an apologetic glance, leaving the drink for me before hustling over to deal with whatever's going on.

Honestly, I don't know what he was thinking by encouraging me to come in. There's no way this place is going to quiet down anytime soon. It's past eight o'clock and well after happy hour, but there are still more and more people streaming in all the time. It's not even a play-off or anything like that—I don't follow sports, I admit, but there aren't any games playing on the TVs sprinkled throughout the establishment.

A few minutes pass before I see him again, and he shrugs in a helpless sort of way while gesturing to the next customer and the next. It's not hard to notice the way the girls lean over the bar, practically putting their boobs out for him to examine. I can't help but roll my eyes either.

My drink is almost finished before he manages to find me again. "I go on break in a few minutes. Sorry, I really didn't expect it to explode like this tonight."

"It's no problem."

Besides, he makes a good drink. He gestures for me to meet him near the kitchen. Good thing he gave me advance warning since it takes me forever to make it back there. I'm not a very pushy person by nature, so it's not easy for me to cut through the dense crowd.

He pulls me in for a quick hug when I reach him. "I'm really sorry," he murmurs in my ear, leaning in close so I can hear him.

"It's okay. Honestly, we can always talk some other time." It doesn't even seem that important anymore, which is a funny sort of conclusion to come to after I practically got trampled back there.

"No, I've been looking forward to seeing you all night." He takes me by the hand and leads me farther back until we reach a door marked *Employees Only*. It doesn't matter to him what the sign says since he opens the door and pulls me into a dimly lit storage room.

"Is this where you normally take your breaks?" I ask with a soft laugh.

"On nights like this, honestly, yeah. I just need to get away from all those people for a minute." He removes the elastic from his hair, letting it fall around his shoulders before running his fingers through it until it looks like a lion's mane. "All that energy pressing in on me, it's draining. I need to guard my own."

"Sure, sure. I get it." I don't really, though I think I understand. It's never easy for me to be around big groups of people for a long time. Maybe that's why … the energy of all those people affects mine. *Huh, never thought of it like that.*

He paces the small, square space, rolling his

head back and forth on his shoulders, shaking out his arms and hands. He takes deep breaths in through the nose, out through the mouth. It's sort of fascinating to watch him do it, though I can't help but feel like I'm intruding. I hang back near a rack of wine bottles and let him do his thing.

A few minutes later, he seems a lot more relaxed and loose. "Okay, what's up? What did you want to talk about?"

Whoops. He just got himself in a nice, relaxed mood, and I'm about to drop this on him.

"Oh, I just wanted to warn you that things might get a little testy with Ashley and the other girls."

He rolls his eyes, letting out a heavy sigh. "What do you mean? What's happening?"

"I know it seems like I'm tattling or something, and I'm not trying to, really. Ashley reached out to me today and warned me about you." I make it a point to keep smiling, treating this like it's a joke.

His eyes narrow. "What's that mean? What did she say?"

"Don't get upset. It's not worth it. Listen, I didn't say this before, but it's pretty obvious most of the girls in the group have a thing for you. You must know that."

He doesn't confirm it verbally, but the way his eyes lower to the floor tells me what I need to know.

"And here I am, an outsider, coming in and getting in their way. I don't take it personally. But I thought you should know that the next time you get together with any of them, they might be annoyed with you for going out with me."

"See? This is exactly the kind of thing I was talking about. I'm so sick of the drama. Like a bunch of little kids. I thought I'd left that behind in college."

I can't help but smile a little to myself since that's exactly what I was thinking while Ashley raked me over the coals. "Yeah, I know. But I guess that's what's going to happen whenever you get a bunch of people together for any extended period of time. Eventually, relationships form, they break up, that sort of thing. Especially around actors."

He scoffs. "What do you mean by that?"

Once again, I can see now how that might've sounded like an insult. "Anybody who lives in their emotions. Artists. That's all I meant."

He accepts this, sighing again, leaning against the closed door with his arms folded. He's wearing a short-sleeved shirt tonight, and I am not unhappy about it. Even now, standing in this little storeroom with him, talking over something that doesn't make either of us particularly happy, I can't help but entertain the notion of running my hands over those thick, smooth arms.

"You would never see anything like this coming from the people you'll meet on Saturday," he assures me. "They're professionals. Not a bunch of kids. It's obvious I need to put some distance between myself and the rest of those children."

"Okay, that's not how I wanted this to go. I'm not trying to cause trouble—"

"This has nothing to do with you. Trust me," he insists when I shoot him a skeptical look. "It's something that's been brewing in me for a long time. Maybe you coming into my life is what I needed to finally get me moving. I don't want to hurt anybody's feelings. I don't want to stir up animosity. That's the last thing I want."

"I believe you."

"I'm just tired of the whispers and the secrets and the backbiting. I've grown beyond them." He frowns, and when his eyes meet mine, I see a lot of doubt in them. "Does that sound shitty? You can tell me if it does. I don't mind."

I shake my head. "Not at all. It was clear from the jump that you're head and shoulders above the rest of them. Don't get me wrong; they were all good, but you were exceptional. From everything you've told me, you take this very seriously. You deserve to be inspired and, I don't know, nurtured by the people you're around. Not feeling like you're being held back or like your personal life is being dissected."

"Honestly? I don't even know how anybody knew we were out together. I didn't tell any of them."

"Maybe it was a guess? We did stand around and chat for a little while after leaving the diner. It wasn't a secret that we were … into each other."

That earns me a wicked grin. "You're probably right," he agrees. "You can't do anything without somebody paying more attention than they should."

"I hate to tell you this, hot stuff, but that's how life is going to go if you want to be a successful actor. People are going to want to know everything about you. You'll be a public commodity."

He huffs at this, shaking his head. "My life is mine."

Poor, naive little boy. He doesn't get it. And frankly, it's not my place to teach him. He'll have to learn the hard way.

"One thing's for sure: I'm not going to be a part of one of these incestuous little families again. Not ever again. Some people get off on the drama but not me." He comes to me, resting his hands on my shoulders. "That's why I pulled back when I was with you. I don't want to keep making the same mistakes, like I said. Hurting people's feelings, getting wrapped up in something I didn't sign up for. It didn't have anything to do with you—I mean, trust me, there was nothing I wanted to do less than leave your apartment."

Maybe it's the way he practically purred it or the way his hands gently massaged my shoulders as he spoke, but I find myself leaning in, straining for even the slightest touch, the barest bit of contact.

"I didn't want you to leave either."

"We'll have to do something about that real

soon."

He takes my chin in one hand and tips it up, planting a soft kiss on my upturned mouth before smiling. "I'd better get back to work. I'm sorry. I wish I could stay here with you all night."

"That makes two of us."

But there's no way for him to avoid having to open the door, looking both ways to make sure nobody notices the fact that I am in there with him before pulling me out of the room.

"We're still on for Saturday night?"

"You bet." I would watch him do just about anything.

Although the fact that there won't be dozens and dozens of people pressing in on me from all directions sweetens the pot quite a bit.

Chapter Twelve

"ARE YOU SURE you don't have time to go out with me tonight? It might be sort of entertaining."

Hayley offers a weak smile from across the table. Between us is our brunch—eggs Benedict for her, banana-oat pancakes for me.

"No offense, but watching a bunch of amateur actors patting themselves on the back for being great at what they do isn't exactly my idea of a good time."

"You're no fun."

"You know that's not true. I'm a helluva good time when I put my mind to it." She takes a sip of her Bloody Mary, eyeing me up with a wide smile. "Look at you. All shiny and excited. It makes me happy to see you this way," she says, but I don't quite believe her. Something's up; she's not the bubbly sidekick I'm used to.

"I wish you looked a little happier," I confess.

It seems like every time I see her, she looks more tired, more drained.

She waves a hand, shaking her head. "I've been burning the midnight oil lately; that's all."

"And here I am, dragging you out for brunch. You should've turned me down. You probably could've used the extra sleep."

"Absolutely not. I won't give up everything about my life just because I'm trying to climb the corporate ladder."

Here's the thing about Hayley: she's very cool, calm, collected—on the outside. Perfect in just about every way. Unflappable.

But I know her. And even she has her little tells. The way she drums her fingers on the table. The way she plays with her glass rather than looking me in the eye.

Suspicion scratches at the back of my mind, and I try to ignore it. It's no use though. I can't shake the feeling that she's hiding something from me, which is unlike her.

Instead of confronting her about it, which would only get us into a fight, I put on my no-nonsense face. "You're gonna make yourself sick, working so hard. I know it's what you have to do right now, but don't forget to take care of yourself."

"Yes, Mommy."

At least she's looking at me again, which I guess is a good sign so I change the subject.

"I'd love for you to meet Rafe. I'm sure you two would hit it off." I spear a piece of pancake with my fork before dragging it through the pool of syrup and popping it into my mouth. Brunch is my big indulgence, where I let myself eat whatever I want without giving myself a hard time about it.

"I don't know. An actor? Truth be told, I could never stand their type."

She's so negative today, which isn't like her.

What the heck is going on?

"I never knew that. I didn't think you had anything against actors."

She shakes her head with a frown. "No, that's not what I mean. Sorry. I have a headache, and it's screwing me up. I don't mix well with big egos; that's all."

"He's not like that. You know I don't suffer egos either."

"That's true."

"He's a nice guy and a terrific actor. I'm sure he has what it takes to make a name for himself."

A tiny smirk tugs at her lips. "You're not just saying that because you're super into him?"

"No."

"Because when we're busy lusting after somebody, we might miss out on the fact that they're not as awesome as we think they are."

"Believe me, he's the real deal. I can't wait to see what he's capable of once he gets around serious actors. Not the people he was with earlier in the week." I automatically scowl when I remember the conversation with Ashley, who hasn't reached out since yesterday. I wonder if anybody knows I met up with Rafe at the bar. I'm sure their heads would explode if they did.

Maybe I'm a bit bitter, but how can I help it? I've never been a fan of people telling me what to do, especially when those people are basically strangers.

"I remember the girls we knew in college who acted the way you described," she muses, stirring what's left of her drink with the celery stalk. "Hanging on a guy, hoping he would eventually see them and know how important and amazing they were. Like, all of a sudden, boom, the veil would lift, and he'd come to his senses."

"Yeah, and in the meantime, they made fools of themselves and were painfully obvious to everybody else. Then again, it's easy for us to say since we're not in the mix. Love makes us do all sorts of things we cringe over afterward."

"It doesn't even take love to make us do that," she murmurs, staring at the glass like it holds the secrets of the universe.

"And the whole incestuous-family thing makes my skin crawl."

She snorts. "Really? It's not literal."

"I know that. But still, I have to admit, it makes me feel a little … icky."

"Anybody we date at this age is bound to have had a bunch of sexual partners before they met us. You realize that, right?"

"It's not the same as being part of a group of people who practically swap partners. I know it's not really that bad, but nobody wants to have it thrown in their face that the person they've just started dating has stuck it in anything that stopped moving long enough to have it stuck in them."

"You're such a poet." She giggles, and I'm glad to see her lightening up a little.

"What can I say? That's why I make the big bucks."

"And you know," she continues, "this sort of thing doesn't only happen in acting groups. It happens all the time. Everywhere. Wherever there are big groups of fairly young people, all together for long periods of time. Working hard to meet a common goal. It creates a sense of intimacy—and fast."

"You sound like you're speaking from experience." I try to make it sound like I'm teasing, but really, I'm concerned. *What is she not telling me?*

She lifts a shoulder. "It's human psychology. That's how we all behave."

"So, you're sure there isn't something you're keeping from me? Hayley, come on. I've known you for a long time. I can tell when you're trying to hide something. You're not good at it. No offense," I add when she frowns.

Her face twitches. Her nostrils flare, her lips drawn together in a fine line. The look of a woman trying to decide whether or not she should say anything. All I can do is sit here and wait.

"Fine. You might as well know." She leans in, arms crossed on the table, her eyes darting back and forth like she's making sure nobody else is listening. "I've been seeing one of the men at the firm."

I practically have to hold on to my chin to keep it from hitting the table. "Are you serious?" I whisper.

This is the last thing I expected. She's always so smart, the girl who has everything together.

"See? This is why I didn't want to say anything."

"I'm not judging you!" I hiss. "It's just that I can't believe you didn't say anything about it to me. How long have you been seeing him?"

"A couple of weeks. Seriously, it's not a big deal."

My best friend has been seeing someone and has gone out of her way not to tell me about it, and she wants me to believe it isn't a big deal. I hate to be the one to tell her she's way off the mark if she thinks I'm going to let this go.

"Who is he? What's his name? What does he do for the firm?"

"He is a senior associate in one of the departments."

A pit forms in my stomach before I even have the chance to give voice to the next logical question. "Your department?"

"Kitty …"

"You can tell me. Of all people in the world, I'm the one you can tell."

It's clear she would rather bite off her tongue

than continue this conversation. On the other hand, she's never been the kind of girl to back down in the face of a challenge. "My department."

In other words, he's pretty much her boss.

I'm feeling like an outsider in my best friend's life.

"Why did you feel like you couldn't tell me?"

She blinks hard before snickering. "This is why. Right here, this is the reason I didn't say anything."

"I don't understand."

"Because I saw the look in your eyes when I said he was in my department."

"Hayley, I'm not judging you. I'm just surprised you didn't tell me."

"Oh, sure. I know that look. You think I'm an idiot. You think I'm putting my career in jeopardy. You think I'm too smart to do this. Well, let me tell you, when you're working long nights and feel that connection with someone, sometimes, you can't help it. You have to give in. A girl has needs, Kitty. Maybe some of us do need the hot sex instead of the sweet connection."

She couldn't have hurt me worse if she'd reached across the table and slapped me.

"Hayley, where is this coming from?"

Her mouth opens and quickly closes. She jumps to her feet and leaves some cash on the table. "Forget it. I'm not going to talk about this in public. I don't even know what to say. But it's not worth it."

"It's worth it to me. You're my best friend." I take her hand before she can walk away, and she pauses for a second. I decide to take that as a good sign. "Hayley, I love you. I'm here for you."

She scoffs ever so softly. "So long as I'm keeping my life as PG as you are, right?" With that, she pulls her hand free and leaves me sitting alone, wondering how everything suddenly went so bad.

Chapter Thirteen

"I WOULDN'T BE too upset about it."

"That's easy for you to say. You didn't have your butt handed to you by your best friend." It's unusual for me to have a beer so early in the day, even on a Saturday, but desperate times call for desperate measures, and this is definitely a desperate time.

Hayley and I haven't had a fight since college, and even then, it was over something stupid. Like who took whose curling iron or something like that.

This? This was real. This was nasty and mean.

At least Matt has the good grace to look like he feels sorry for me. "It's hard when you fight with a friend, especially when you're as close as you and Hayley are."

"Honestly, it's like I didn't even know who I was talking to. She never hits below the belt like that."

"You said she's under a lot of stress right now." Meanwhile, it's as if his body reacts to the word stress by stretching out, relaxing even more deeply than it already was. He crosses his ankles, his heels on top of his coffee table.

Phoebe is curled up at his side, and they're watching me walk back and forth.

If I were in a better frame of mind, it might be kind of cute, the way their heads move in sync. Back and forth, back and forth, following my progress.

"Sure, I figured all that stress came from work." Now, I know it also comes from a secret affair with her boss.

"My point is, she's not thinking rationally. She's tired, burned out. I'm sure if this had happened at any other time, when her life was a little calmer, she wouldn't have said those things."

"I wish I could believe that."

"I'm just saying, I'm a pretty smart guy. I'm usually right about mostly everything."

I shouldn't laugh, but I do. "Don't get too full of yourself, okay?"

"Too late for that."

"Yeah, I know."

But I don't mind. Far from it. He doesn't have to sit there and listen to me freaking out over a rare fight with my best friend. He didn't have to offer me a beer either.

"Friends fight like this all the time. Did I ever tell you about the fight I had with my buddy Josh? It was over some girl we were both into. Turned out, she wasn't into either of us, but we hadn't known that at the time. He ended up punching me right in the jaw." He rubs his jaw with a rueful grin.

"No way!"

"Yes way."

"And what did you do?"

"Once I stopped seeing stars, I hit him back. What else was I supposed to do? We both had our tempers up."

"That's awful, losing your friendship over a girl who didn't even want either of you."

"We didn't lose our friendship. I never said that."

It surprises me enough to stop me in my tracks. "How the heck can you still be friends with somebody who punched you?"

He shrugs, which only surprises me more. "You get over it. Guys are like that. We can fight, even throw fists, but we get it out of our system. It's not like it is with women."

I fold my arms, staring down at him. This is not the time to be making generalizations like that. "What does that mean? How is it with women?"

"Forget I ever said anything."

"Too late for that."

"Don't bite my head off. I'm just saying, women tend to project. Guys don't do that. We admit our feelings and move on. If one of us takes a hit for it, so be it. If it happens to be with a good friend, then it's worth the effort to get the bad blood out of the way, clear the air, and move on."

He makes it sound so simple. In reality, it feels

anything but simple.

"I just don't know how we're going to come back from this. She made me sound so judgy and awful. I didn't think I was."

He heaves a sigh. "You're not. You really aren't. And you know I would tell you if I thought there was a grain of truth to what she said. I don't sugarcoat things."

"No, heaven forbid."

This earns me a smirk.

"Like I was saying, I wouldn't tell you something if I didn't believe it. And from what you've told me, it sounds a lot like Hayley feels guilty about what she's doing more than anything else. She just pushed it on you to make herself feel better."

It's not often that Matt makes me stop and think. Normally, I'm too busy reminding myself not to smack him to put much thought into the things he says.

Granted, now that I know he thinks it's a good thing to be smacked sometimes, I might not work so hard to control the impulse to do so.

"So, what you're saying is, she was only lashing out?" It's almost hard to believe the warmth that stirs to life in my chest. Like I was only waiting for a tiny bit of hope to grab on to.

"Of course! She's not a stupid girl. She knows the kind of trouble she can get into—and the same goes for this guy she's sleeping with."

"Yeah, I mean, he's her boss, for crying out loud. How could he put both of their jobs in jeopardy like that? Do you think he's just using her?"

"Maybe. There's a reason they say you shouldn't shit where you eat."

"Seriously, I'm worried about her."

"I hope, if anyone, he's the one who would get caught; I don't want her to get into trouble."

"Neither do I. Now, I wish I could get ahold of this guy and shake some sense into him." My hands tighten around the bottle.

"Easy now. I don't want Phoebe cutting her paws on broken glass." He stands, working the bottle out of my hands. It was empty anyway.

I watch as he takes it to the kitchen and tosses it into the recycling bin.

"She probably figured I would judge whoever it is, didn't she?"

"Of course. Like I said, she's no dummy. She knows what she's doing. She's gotta feel guilty about it on some level. That's really why she didn't tell you; I'd bet anything on it."

I rub my arms, shivering a little. "I can't believe she was so quick to jump on the attack, you know? She's usually so supportive of me. It hurt my feelings that she didn't think I'd do the same for her."

He's frowning when he returns to the living room with a fresh beer for each of us. I would normally refuse, but this is a two-beer sort of situation.

"Yeah, and I'm sure she feels bad for saying it. We don't mean the things we say when we're angry, Kitty. You know that."

I sink to the floor, sitting cross-legged. Phoebe takes this as an invitation to join me, not that I mind. Stroking her soft fur goes a long way toward calming me down.

"I wish there were a way to show her I'm still here for her and not being judgy in any way."

He sits on the couch, elbows on his knees, giving me a funny sort of smile as he leans over to pat Phoebe's head. "Which is exactly why you aren't the sort of friend she described. Even now, when you're miserable and your feelings are hurt, all you can think about is her. How much you want to make everything better."

He's being so nice today. Maybe I should come to him with friendship troubles more often.

No, it has to be his new girlfriend.

"Dating suits you."

He bursts out laughing. "What does that have to do with anything?"

"I don't know. You're so much nicer. Not that you were ever really mean, but you're, like ... mellow, you know?"

"I don't think anyone's ever called me mellow before."

"Well, how frequently do you seriously date somebody?"

"Good point."

"Whoever she is, she must be a miracle worker or a saint or something. Is that it? She gunning for sainthood?"

"Now that you mention it, she does wear a nun's habit around the house, but I figured it was a comfort thing."

I can't come up with a retort, so all I do is roll my eyes. "How can you stand living with him, Phoebe? Doesn't it all get to be too much after a while?"

All she does is look at me with those great big eyes of hers, and I have no choice but to give her a hug.

"How are things going with Man Bun?"

A snarky comment almost trips off my tongue before I can stop it, but I manage in time. "Why did you call him that?"

"It's not exactly an insult."

"It's not a compliment either, not the way you meant it. But that's not what I mean. How did you know he has long hair?" I know I haven't described him. In fact, this is the first time we've talked since I met Rafe.

His face goes slack for a second, and I swear, his cheeks flush just a little. But that might be a trick of the light. "You're going to make a big deal out of this."

"Out of what?"

"When he was leaving the other night, I was just

getting in. I swear, I had literally just stepped into my apartment and closed the door when I heard your door open. So, I looked out the peephole. I wanted to get a look at this guy."

"You're such a sneak!"

"Don't even pretend you've never done the same thing. I know you have. I could hear you breathing on the other side of the door one time when I was saying good-bye to somebody after she spent the night. Don't bother lying," he warns before I have the chance to say anything.

He's right. I did watch that one time. Mostly because I wanted to get a look at the sort of girl he brought home with him. I'd never seen any of them before. I'd only heard them hollering like all get-out.

Truth be told, I had been a little jealous on more than one occasion. All I had known about him at that point in time was how hot he was. I didn't know he was also such a pest.

"Well, now, you got a look at him. Congratulations."

He snickers. "It was the thrill of my life, let me tell you."

"I'm going to see him perform tonight. I'm looking forward to it. He's really good."

"How would you know whether he was good or not? Have you studied acting?"

"No, genius, but I've watched a million movies. And I've seen bad acting. Heck, I saw some bad acting that night. I might not be able to act, but I know good acting when I see it. Trust me, you'll see his name in lights one day."

"I'm sure you felt the same way about your sweetheart Dustin before he showed his true colors."

"No comment," I growl.

"I wonder if they'll make him cut off his man bun when he makes it to Hollywood."

"I'm glad you're so pleased with yourself right now. I really am. Maybe if you got to know him a little better, you would see he's a nice person. Hey!" The idea strikes me so suddenly and so hard that, for some reason, my hand shoots out, and I smack him on the leg. "We should all get together! The four of us! I would love to meet your girlfriend."

"Oh, I'm sure you would."

"What? I really want to. I would like to know about her and see if she's, you know, the right sort of girl for you."

"And you're such an expert on the subject?"

"Listen, you think of me as a little sister, and I think of you as a brother. Why wouldn't I want to get a look at the girl you're dating?"

He frowns, his brows drawing together. "I don't know. Maybe. We'll see."

"I won't embarrass you."

"The fact that you feel the need to say that should explain why I'm not jumping at the idea." He laughs.

Chapter Fourteen

WELL …

This is certainly different.

Instead of a cramped little space with black walls and black floors and a heating system that doesn't work, Rafe's directions have brought me to a cozy studio above a trendy-looking art gallery. The place is bright, warm, clean. Does somebody live here? I guess it's possible. Maybe they moved the furniture out of the way to make room.

Already, a handful of people are walking around, chatting quietly over drinks. Rafe spots me the second I walk in, and I couldn't be happier. I've never been great at making small talk with strangers.

"Hey you." His hug is strong, tight, and I wish he wouldn't let me go.

I can't help but remember the heat between us at my apartment. I want to go back to that feeling. *Hmmm.*

Especially when he kisses me. It's a chaste, we're-in-public kiss, but it still makes my knees weak.

"This is so nice," I whisper, accepting a glass of wine when he hands it to me.

"Jonah's awesome. This is the space we always work in. He lives upstairs and uses this floor for his art and performances and such." He gestures to the walls, on which are hanging numerous, bold paintings and blown-up photos.

"How cool." I admire a few of the works before turning to him and murmuring, "So, is Jonah the person who leads the group?"

"Yeah, I guess so. We're all friends of his in one way or another. He only invites people he thinks have a shot at a future."

Does he know how he glows when he talks like this? I can see that he's proud of himself. And he should be. He works hard, and others pick up on that.

He waves to a man who just entered. "Hey, I want you to meet my agent. I didn't know he was gonna show tonight." With my hand in his, Rafe leads me to the man who's now taking off his coat and scarf.

"You must be Kitty." He takes my hand in both of his when I extend it to shake. "Rafe's told me a lot about you. I'm Bill Watson."

"Considering Rafe and I met a week ago, I'm interested to know what he could've told you." I laugh. "It's nice to meet you."

Now, I remember him. He was at the workshop. The girls peeled away from me, so they could say hi to him. No wonder they were so happy to see him there. He's a real-deal sort of agent, if I remember correctly. The sort of agent everybody's jealous of Rafe for having.

A woman calls out to Rafe, waving him over.

"I'm sorry. I have to see what that's about." He leans down to kiss my cheek and then whispers, "You're in good hands. He only looks imposing."

Imposing? He looks downright ferocious, wearing a slick suit and a flashy watch. "I just came from a string of meetings today," he explains before taking a glass of wine waiting on the bar.

"Pardon me?"

"You were looking at my suit. I don't usually dress up for events like this."

I have to laugh at myself. "I hope I wasn't ogling you too much. I don't get out among people all that often."

"You're too busy writing, right?" He winks, putting me at ease. "Don't think I didn't look you up. Impressive. Very impressive."

"It was all luck." I shrug.

"No such thing. I mean it," he insists when I grimace, skeptical. "Luck is nothing more than preparation meeting opportunity. Sure, sometimes, a person gets discovered. They're in the right place at the right time, but if they don't have what it takes, what good does it do them?"

He looks me up and down, his dark eyes flickering over me. "You must've worked hard on that first book for it to hit the way it did. I bet you stayed in when all your friends were out, partying and drinking and getting laid, right?"

My, oh my. He and Maggie would get along so well.

For all I know, they know each other.

For all I know, he's the ex-husband she sometimes mentions. But, no, he's younger than her. Late forties at most.

"Wow, it's like you were there."

He chuckles, touching my elbow and steering me out of the way of a couple approaching the bar. I normally would flinch away from that sort of gesture, but somehow, it's okay. He has a winning nature, I guess, and I don't get a smarmy feeling from him.

"That's my point," he continues once we've moved. "You worked hard. You were prepared. It just so happened that an opportunity opened up. Your publisher was looking for a fresh, new voice. Someone young, somebody who'd inject life into their backlist. Because you had already done the work, you were there when they were looking for someone like you. Never discount that. I mean it."

"I won't."

I wouldn't dare go against anything this man says. His intensity is staggering but not in a bad way. Instead, it makes me want to buckle down and keep working hard.

"And don't discount your talent. Never discount that. Writing can be taught, of course. The fundamentals of grammar, symbolism, showing instead of telling, etcetera." He waves a hand, making his shiny watch glimmer in the soft overhead lighting. "But what can't be created is a storyteller. You've gotta have it here." He taps his chest, nodding sagely.

It's like he's freaking Yoda or something. Only human. And he talks in regular sentences.

"Do you represent writers? Because I could be in the market for a new agent." I laugh, thinking of Lois.

Poor Lois. I love her dearly, but the woman falls asleep in the middle of meetings and barely has two words to say to me at a time. She used to be sharp and ruthless, but I'm not so sure she can deliver anymore. She should have told me about the backlog and assured me everything was going to be okay before Maggie called me. I'm disappointed that I still can't get her on the phone, but maybe I just need to drop it for now. I know what Maggie wants me to do, and I've been working on it. Maybe it isn't worth starting an argument with my agent. Maybe I shouldn't have asked that.

He laughs with me and then shakes his salt-and-pepper head. "No, sorry to say. I'd love to represent you. We could have your books turned into blockbusters like that." He snaps his fingers.

"Oh well. At least you're putting Rafe out there, so the world can see how talented he is."

"He is, isn't he?" His entire demeanor changes.

His expression softens, and his eyes shine. "He's the real deal, that kid. You saw him at the workshop last week, right? I remember seeing you there."

"Yes, that's where we met."

"He's head and shoulders above all of them, putting it mildly." He shrugs. "Sorry if you're good friends with anybody else there."

"No, not really. Believe me, Rafe's the one who left a lasting impression on me," I assure him, my head bobbing up and down. "He's in a whole other league."

"I was the one who steered him toward Jonah. I know Rafe can become something big if he's around the right people. People who challenge him and help him grow. Sure, he's a big shot in that piddly little group, but that won't get him anything but a stroked ego. Among other things." He winces. "There I go again with my mouth."

I have to laugh though. "Hey, I write romance for a living. I can handle it." Even though my skin crawls a little at the reminder that Rafe's been around the block.

"That's not entirely what I meant." He looks across the room, where Rafe is loosening up along with the other actors.

There are ten of them in all, and I can tell right away that this is a next-level experience. They all take it seriously and move like dancers. So graceful and fluid, completely in control of their bodies.

"What did you mean?"

"I mean, once he hits it big, it'll be tough to keep the fans away from him. I know Rafe. He's a good kid. But it'll take a special woman to handle any jealousy that might come up. Especially in a town like Hollywood."

Talk about a record-scratch moment. My eyes go wide. "What are you talking about? He's going to Hollywood?"

"Shh." He throws a quick, panicked look to Rafe, but he's still warming up. "I haven't talked about it with him yet. I just came from a meeting with the producers. I got him an audition for a horror film in LA."

"No way!" I clutch his arm, shocked and happy.

"It's not for another few weeks, but yes. They watched his reel and loved him. They think he'll make a great lead."

"That's fantastic!"

"I was going to tell him after the performances tonight. I didn't want to throw him. Even if this is just a showcase, he takes it seriously."

"I can tell," I murmur, watching as the actors finish their warm-ups.

"So, you know, if the two of you become a couple, you'll have that to wrestle with. Rafe's as loyal as the day is long, but fans? They'll stop at nothing."

I'm about to open my mouth to remind him that Rafe and I just met.

"Oh, it looks like they're about to start."

I quickly follow Bill and take a seat next to him.

What a note to leave our conversation on. I try to focus on the performance and keep my mind from drifting, but then I think ... Do I want to a long-term relationship with Rafe?

Chapter Fifteen

"I COULD FLY right now. Seriously." Rafe's entire face glows.

After his performance, Bill shared the news with him about the audition, and now, he's lighting up my apartment with his signature smile.

"It's so exciting!" I nudge him with a grin. "A Hollywood audition. I couldn't be happier for you."

"It's like everything's happening all at once. I mean, it's surreal. I meet you and then get this audition." He pauses in the middle of his salad we brought up from a restaurant down the street, and he looks at me. "It's just crazy, right?"

What am I supposed to say to that? I wish I knew what he was looking for.

"Yes, but it sounds like you have put a lot of work into your art, and now, you have an extraordinary chance to show off your talent. I'm just a bonus." We both laugh. "Just keep a positive mindset, and I'm sure you'll do a terrific job at the audition."

"You're right. Absolutely." He goes back to his salad while I go back to mine.

He can't keep the grin off his face—and I don't want him to. Frankly, it's adorable to see him so excited like this.

How is it that I like him so much when we've hardly known each other for a week? Am I completely out of my mind for thinking so highly of him when I barely know the first thing about him? Am I asking for trouble?

"Thank you." He shoots me a shy smile that makes him look ten years younger.

Oh yeah, girls are going to be swooning over that face of his when it's on the big screen.

"For what?"

"For being happy for me."

I give him an incredulous look.

"No, let me explain." He turns to face me, the salad forgotten for now. "The last few girls I dated were actors, like me. All basically at the same level—some regional stuff, maybe a decent production here or there. But nothing impressive, you know?"

"Sure."

"It's like a competition all the time. Like, I wouldn't feel right going to them and being happy over scoring an audition out in LA because I'd know they'd be jealous. Even if they pretended not to be, I'd be able to see it. When I was in Philly and word got out that I was nominated for a Barrymore, my girlfriend at the time broke up with me."

"You're kidding!"

"Not even a little bit," he sighs with a shrug. "It

took five days before she packed up her stuff and left. She couldn't stand being around me anymore. Said I had a big head. All because I'd gotten nominated for an award. Hell, I didn't even win. I heard from mutual friends that she cheered and clapped when she heard I hadn't won."

"Ew! What a jerk!"

He laughs. "I love the way you put things. Yeah, that was a jerk thing to do."

"I'm sorry you didn't feel supported back then."

He takes one of my hands, lifting it to his lips and placing the softest kiss on my knuckles. I didn't know before now that it was possible to get turned on by such a slight kiss, but here we are. The fact that he holds my gaze the entire time only makes me want to jump him even more.

"I feel supported now, which is what matters." He kisses my hand again before letting go. "So, what did you think of Bill?"

"I think he has your best interests at heart, which is saying something for an agent."

"I guess you know a lot about that."

"I've heard stories of people getting screwed over, yeah. I bet you have too."

"I know I'm absolutely lucky to have him in my corner. He goes to bat for me time and again—well, you know, you've seen it for yourself. I'm sure those producers didn't care to hear about some nobody from New York. He works his ass off."

"You deserve an agent who'll do that for you."

"He likes you a lot. I can tell. That's high praise."

"I'm flattered." Though I would like to know what this has to do with kissing me, which is what I wish he'd do right now. We can talk later.

But no, he's still too keyed up over Bill's announcement. "LA. An audition for a movie. A real movie too, not some student film. I can't tell you how many of those I've done, and they never go anywhere."

"It's so fancy. I'll be able to say I know somebody who auditioned in LA." I put my hand over my chest and bat my eyelashes. "I'll be able to say I knew you when you were tending bar."

"And I'm able to say I know someone who's written best sellers," he teases. "Don't forget how fancy you are."

"Not so fancy. Look around. You don't see any paparazzi outside my apartment. I think I like that too. The anonymity. I have to be honest. I don't know if I could stand being recognized by everybody on the street. I'd lock myself away."

"Like Greta Garbo," he muses.

"Oh, my grandmother was a huge fan of hers and used to see her on the street all the time," I tell him with a grin. "It was like a sport in Manhattan for a long time—Garbo sightings. I can understand why she was so reclusive. I don't think I could ever live up to that image. Because it's all fake."

"I think some people forget that," he muses,

picking through what's left of his food. "They start listening to their own press and forget they're just people. That's when trouble starts. I know actors on Broadway who have that problem too. They get all wrapped up in how fabulous they are."

"I would hate to see that happen to you," I murmur, watching him.

"I don't think that'll happen to me. I need good friends in my corner though, reminding me I'm plain old Rafe whenever I start getting a big head."

"Then, I guess you don't want to hear that I've based the hero of my current book on you, huh?"

He drops his fork into the container and turns to me. "What? No way."

"I mean, he has a different name—it's Ryder right now, though that might change—but otherwise, he's a lot like you."

"You're kidding! It's not like anybody else would know, but that's still the coolest thing!" He sits back against the cushions with a goofy grin. "The hero in a romance novel. That's not the kind of thing that happens every day."

"I was afraid you'd think it was corny."

"Not even a little bit. Come here." He pulls me to him, and before I know it, I'm straddling his lap. "Anybody who'd think that was corny is missing something in their brain. I think it's cool. And you know I have to read it when you're finished."

"Of course. I'd hope you would."

His hands slide up and down my arms as his

voice drops to barely a whisper. "Will your characters have a happy ending?"

"That's the whole idea," I whisper back with a
grin. "A happily ever after is guaranteed. I wish life
were that simple, don't you?"

"It can be."

He's now tracing my spine, and, oh boy, I want
to purr like a cat and arch my back. I don't know
how it's possible that such a simple touch can make
me feel this way, but again, here we are, and I'm
about two seconds away from grinding against his
legs like a dog in heat.

"I can tell you what would make me happy
right now."

"What would that be?" I ask, though I'm pretty
sure I have an idea.

His hands press flat against my back as he pulls
me in until our torsos are flush. I'm breathless all of
a sudden, lost in his eyes and the heat between us. I
don't think I've ever met anybody as good and
decent as him and with such a good head on his
shoulders.

And he's opened me up to an entirely new way
of thinking about my work too. I'm excited about it
for the first time in a long time, and I owe that to
him.

"What do you think?" His smile is knowing,
teasing, and I practically melt under it.

"I thought you wanted to take things slow." It's
a struggle to speak, I swear, with his hands now

cupping my butt the way they are.

"I do. But that was an entire five days ago, too, and I know you so much better now." He moves in to inhale the scent of my hair and skin, making me close my eyes as his lips skim my jaw.

"Don't tell me you can't control yourself around me. I can't believe that's true."

"Why not?" He pulls back a little, searching my face with those two pools of ice blue. "Don't you know how devastating attractive you are?"

"No." I giggle. "Not even close."

"Oh, Kitty, Kitty." He shakes his head with a soft growl. "You have no idea then. You could make a monk reconsider his vows."

I mean, what am I even supposed to do besides wrap my arms around his neck and kiss him harder than I've ever kissed anybody in my entire life? What would any sane, red-blooded person do in a situation like this?

Just when I'm sure this is about to head for the bedroom, a knock at the door bursts the perfect little lust bubble we've built around ourselves.

And I know who it has to be.

"Damn it," I whisper, sagging in Rafe's arms. My sweater is halfway up, and his hands are underneath. *For Pete's sake, could I get a break just this once?*

"Who is it?" he rasps in my ear.

"My neighbor. He's the only person who would knock."

Especially since my best friend isn't talking to me. The thought of Hayley is like a bucket of ice water being poured over my head, which kills any hope of the mood sparking to life again.

"I'm sorry," I whisper before climbing off his lap, straightening my clothes and hair on my way to the door. "I'm coming!" I call out.

Matt is waiting, Phoebe beside him, when I open the door. He instantly sizes me up and then looks over my shoulder. "Oh. I'm interrupting something."

"You could say that." I lower my voice to a whisper. "I told you I was going out tonight."

"I forgot."

"It's been, like, eight hours."

"I know that. What do you want me to say? I'm not used to you going out." He glances down at the dog, who looks up at him. "And you said you'd watch her if I had to leave for the night."

"You could have your girlfriend over every once in a while, you know. Just saying."

"How do you know I don't?" he counters with a raised eyebrow.

"Has your technique suddenly lessened? Or is she just really quiet?"

He snickers. "Okay, fine. I'm running late as it is. Would you mind?"

"What's this all about?" Rafe joins us, standing behind me.

I can practically feel the tension.

This is tiresome. And not the first time I've been through it. Every guy I've dated who meets Matt automatically assumes he's a threat. Even Rafe, it seems, and here I thought he might actually be above that sort of behavior.

Men will be men, I guess. I wonder if Matt would take the same philosophical stance as earlier today when he told me guys would hit each other to get rid of bad blood and then be friends after.

Something tells me he wouldn't.

"I'm dog-sitting for the night. Right, sweetheart?" I pat my knees, and she comes to me, tail wagging. "We're gal pals. This is Phoebe."

"Matt." Matt extends his hand. "Neighbor."

"Rafe." He doesn't bother explaining who he is.

I don't even know what he'd say if he tried. *Guy who was just about to get it on with Kitty?* I mean, it's sort of long, and it might make for an even more uncomfortable situation.

"Well, thanks for the help. I'll be back tomorrow morning." Matt gives Rafe a chin jerk, that universal man signal, before strolling down the hall.

Rafe doesn't bother trying to silence his grumbling as Phoebe darts for the coffee table, where our forgotten salads are too good for her to ignore. I scurry after her to shoo her away from the food and she plops down beside me. "I'd better get going. Bill said he'd email me the sides for my audition. I can't wait to get started."

"Sides?"

"Yea, they're small sections of the script for me to practice my part."

"Oh, I see. Do you really have to go right now? Phoebe won't be a bother."

"Yeah, I think it's best."

"I'm sorry. Do you not like dogs?" I ask with a sinking heart while Phoebe practically beats me to death with her wagging tail.

"No, that's not it. I like dogs. She's sweet." Rafe grabs his coat and walks to the door.

He's definitely in a mood now. I decide to let him go without making an issue of it.

"Okay, goodnight then," I say as Phoebe and I see him out the door and watch him walk down then stairs before closing it.

"If your dad thinks I won't make an issue of this, he has another thing coming," I huff and stomp off to my bedroom with Phoebe in tow. From now on, a text or a note slipped under the door will have to suffice. I can always check on Phoebe and bring her over when I'm done doing whatever it is I'm doing.

Though something tells me he deliberately brought her over when he did, the jerk.

Chapter Sixteen

As I WALK into the café, it occurs to me that this is the third time in less than two weeks that I've walked into a situation without any idea of what I'm getting myself into.

The first two times, I was walking into a night of performances.

Now, I'm walking into this writing group, and my knees are knocking like it's my first day out in public. Ever.

My first impression: I spent too much time on my clothes, hair, and makeup. One guy is wearing loud, mismatched socks. There's a woman wearing a woven poncho that looks like it's made primarily of cat fur.

Not a great start.

Still, I take a seat at the edge of the cluster of chairs and smile at the people around me. There are fifteen in all, and each person is holding at least a few pages in their hands. I guess they expect to either exchange pieces or read them aloud.

I didn't bring anything, mostly because I didn't want to insert myself into a group when I'm only just showing up for the first time.

And let's face it. Until I know what these folks are all about, I'm not going to show them my work. It's a personal thing. Sure, the entire world might read what I have to say once it's edited and polished up and what have you, but that's different.

For one thing, I wouldn't be sitting in front of them while they did it. Slowly curling up on myself and wishing I could melt into the floor.

"Welcome, everybody." Leanne, the group's leader and the woman I chatted with online after reaching out, stands in the center of the clustered chairs. We're in the back of the café, away from the regular customers. She keeps her voice low but loud enough for us to hear. "Thanks to all of you for taking the time to be here this week. We have a newcomer this evening, as you might have noticed by now. And it's a real treat to have her here too. Miss Kitty Valentine."

All eyes immediately turn to me, and I could just about die. I give them a little wave and remind myself this is why I don't do public gatherings. My skin is itchy, I'm sweating, and I don't know what to do with my hands.

"Kitty, as you might or might not know, is a published author whose first book was an instant best seller." Leanne beams like she personally discovered me. "I'm sure she'd love to share some tricks of the trade at the end of our session tonight."

Um, no. No, thank you. I did not sign up for that.

Leanne and I need to have a little talk.

But there's no time for that before she starts inviting people to step up and read their work. I sure do wish they'd stop looking at me. All of a sudden, it feels like they're auditioning for me. Like I'm going to offer critiques.

Being put on the spot is not what I came here for.

At least the writing itself is good. One by one, they get up and read really beautiful prose. The sort of prose that, in some cases, I wish I were writing. Lush, lyrical. One of the women talks about the simple act of eating a peach, and I swear, I can almost taste it by the time she's done.

In other words, some of these people are putting me to shame. I'm glad I didn't bring my work with me. They'd laugh me out of the café.

And once each piece is finished, a handful of people give their impressions, their notes. They discuss metaphors and symbols, themes and archetypes. It's stimulating, I'll say that much. I could sit here all night and listen.

But dang it. I'm in way over my head, aren't I? These are real, serious writers who have MFAs and who've traveled the world just to sit where Hemingway and Fitzgerald and Tolstoy once sat, who've dedicated their lives to shaping new worlds using words.

Whereas I've written about fluffy romance and steamy sex.

Talk about a dichotomy here.

"Now, if Kitty would like to say anything, I'm sure we'd all be thrilled to hear it." Leanne waves me up, smiling from ear to ear in a tense sort of way that might actually be a grimace now that I'm standing a little closer and I have a better look at her. She doesn't want me to turn her down after she ran her mouth before asking me if it was okay.

Which, in case I haven't already made it clear, it's not.

I tuck my hair behind my ears and twist my hands in front of me because, once again, I have no idea what to do with them. I'm not prepared for this. "Uh, hi," I offer when I reach her side. "I'm Kitty, as Leanne told you. I have several published books on the market and am in the process of writing my next book right now. I have to admit, I'm at a loss for what I could tell you tonight aside from offering my appreciation of your work. Truly, you've all inspired me to keep going and level up."

I see a few bobbing heads, but for the most part, the group looks expectant—verging on disappointed. Like I was going to offer the keys to the kingdom. Darn this Leanne person, who I notice scurried off for a cup of tea the moment she was able to get free.

"Who's your publisher?" one of the men asks.

"Flagship." This earns me a few approving nods and murmurs. "I've been with them since the beginning. And don't get me wrong. Things haven't

143

always been smooth sailing. One thing I've learned in the last year is how to be flexible and course correct when the time comes for it."

"Can you elaborate?" the poncho lady asks.

"Well, when there are changes in the market and the public knows what they like, your publisher might come to you and ask that you modify your writing a little. As a writer, you might react defensively. Your work is meaningful to you, so you can't imagine going about it any other way. But it's important to maintain a sense of distance too."

"What does that mean? How would you suggest we go about that?" Poncho insists. For a writer, she's not great at understanding words.

"It's easier said than done," I admit. "I got good and drunk the day my editor told me I had to alter my approach."

A few people choke on their laughter, and I realize that maybe I shouldn't have said that. Too late now.

"I got over it though," I add once the laughter quiets. "I had to. If you're anything like me, this is all you can imagine yourself doing for the rest of your life. It's all you want. But our work has to sell in order to make a profit for the publisher and for us, which means it has to appeal to what the public wants."

"What are you writing now, after your publisher asked you to change course?"

"I write romance."

Silence.

Dead silence.

Profound. The silence is profound.

"A romance writer?" Poncho snorts.

Leanne wanders over with her tea. "Yes, Kitty Valentine is a best-selling romance author, of course."

"You brought a romance writer in to tell us what we should do with our careers?" The man who asked laughs behind his hand. He doesn't even try to hold it back or be kind about it. He flat-out laughs.

This was such a good idea. Why don't I branch out more often?

It would be so satisfying, reminding these people that one of us actually has a career. I want to so much. Just for the moment of understanding that I know would cross their faces.

Instead, I clear my throat and look out over all of them. "Romance is a billion-dollar industry. Writing it isn't easier than anything any one of you writes. And if you don't think romance readers are savvy and will hold you to high standards, I dare you to write a romance based on what you think one should be and see what happens."

I then gather every last scrap of my dignity and get the heck out as fast as my feet will carry me.

What was I thinking? I should've known they wouldn't take me seriously. I need to find a romance writer group—if I even bother doing anything like this ever again, which I have to admit, might not happen. *Why should I put myself through that sort of humiliation again if I don't have to?*

It's so easy to forget sometimes, how so-called legit writers look down on my genre. They don't get it. Romance novels are part of what got me through the early days after losing my parents. No, I probably shouldn't have been reading that sort of stuff at such a young age, but I had to turn to something.

I know there are readers out there who look to my books the way I looked to the ones I read back then and to so many other books from that genre. They're a lifeline. That's what some people will never understand.

My phone buzzes as I walk through the park. Okay, more like stomp through the park because I'm really irritated at those snobby people back there.

Rafe texted me. *How's it going?*

Right, because he knew I was going to be there tonight. Because this was all his big stinking idea.

No, I can't do that. It isn't his fault. And if he's working hard on not repeating the same old mistakes, I can do the same. The old Kitty would've pouted and blamed it on Rafe for "making" her go to the meeting.

Not the new Kitty.

But I'm not dumb enough to text while walking through the park at night. A girl has to keep her head up, aware of her surroundings. I choose to call him instead. Even if he's busy, I can leave a voice mail.

He picks up though. "Uh-oh. Couldn't have gone well if I'm getting a call."

"I hope I'm not interrupting anything."

"Nah. Just working on the sides for the audition." I can hear the smile in his voice, and my heart lightens a little.

"Well, it was a disaster back there." I give him the quick-and-dirty rundown, including the way some of those snobby people laughed when they found out what I wrote.

"You've gotta be kidding me! They're a bunch of amateurs and wannabes, and they have the nerve to laugh at you? Who the fuck do they think they are?"

That was exactly what I needed to hear, delivered exactly how I needed to hear it.

"I don't know. I guess they can make themselves feel better for never having published anything by snickering at me. Like, at least they didn't have to stoop this low."

"Kitty, don't let that get to you. You have talent, and you live a good life. An honest life. You're not out there, prostituting yourself to survive or whatever they think of you. Sometimes, people get a little too full of themselves when they talk about their art."

Funny, since I spent an evening watching him interact with fancy, dedicated actors who swanned around Jonah's studio and talked about their process, but I'll let it go. "Yeah, they do. I should've known better. Really. I should've looked for romance writers specifically. They're my people."

"Yeah, they are. You'll know better next time. And they'll lose their minds when they meet you."

"Hmm. I don't know if I want anybody to lose their mind." I giggle. The fact that I'm even considering giggling is a small miracle, all thanks to him.

"You're the best. Fuck those wannabes. I hope your next book is a best seller, and I hope it sits in the front window of every bookstore in Manhattan."

"From your lips to God's ears and all that." Now that I'm feeling better, I can think along other lines—lines that have nothing to do with writing. "So, um, when are we going to see each other again?"

"Can't get enough of me, can you?"

"Something like that."

He's painfully close to the truth. My dreams have been filled with nothing but him night after night—and sadly, all I can do right now is imagine what things would be like if and when we ever have the chance to take our relationship all the way.

Just my luck, time and again, something's always getting in the way.

"I'm working with one of the people you met at Jonah's later tonight; he's helping me with my sides and giving me pointers. And I'm working the next three nights after that. What about Sunday? I'm free all day."

"Great!"

"And maybe we can run lines before we do anything else?"

"Great." I might not be quite as enthused this time, but it's okay. It's better than okay.

He has a lot riding on this audition. Besides, I'd like to get a look at the material he'll be performing.

I'd like to get a look at a lot more than that, but that pretty much goes without saying at this point.

Chapter Seventeen

MY APARTMENT IS you-could-eat-off-the-floor level of clean.

I'm wearing a brand-new top and jeans, and I took great pains with my hair and makeup, so I'd look fantastic but casual.

Needless to say, my underwear is brand-new and sexy. The sort of thing a girl doesn't wear for just anyone.

And I'm sitting on my sofa, watching Rafe as he warms up to run lines. I thought running lines meant just that. Going back and forth, making sure everything's down pat. Evidently, there's a lot I don't know.

"What are you doing now?" I ask, trying to bite back a smile.

"Getting myself loose." He shakes out his hands and then his arms. One leg and then the other. "Have to get my instrument ready."

At first, I snicker because … well, because I have the maturity of a teenage boy.

"What's funny?" He stops his weird shakey-outey thing long enough to frown at me.

Oh. That wasn't supposed to be a joke. He's talking about his body, not his genitals.

"I'm sorry. Don't pay attention to me."

"Okay." He continues tilting his head from side to side, loosening up his neck. "I'm trying to get in the zone, so gimme a minute."

"No problem."

What do I know? Actors have all sorts of things they do to get in the mood, I guess.

Which makes me wonder if I should have a special set of things I do to get in the mood to write. I've never thought about it before now. *Should I create a ritual? Lighting candles, putting positive mantras out into the universe? Something?*

"I am a big brown bear. I am a big brown bear." Rafe walks around in a wide circle, still shaking out his hands and arms, rolling his head from one side to the other. "There's a bee in the tree, and his name is Henri."

Now, this is just too much. Am I not supposed to laugh at this? It's not just the silly things he's saying either. It's the almost-scary way he's moving his entire face. Like speaking is suddenly a full-face activity. His eyes are wide, he keeps moving his jaw back and forth, he's over-enunciating just about everything. He didn't even act this way at Jonah's intimate soiree, or whatever it was meant to be, surrounded by serious actors.

It's better to keep my head down and not look at him. I'll check out the script instead.

It looks like there's no way for me to safely handle this situation though since the first few lines of the scene we'll be rehearsing are like something out of a cheesy horror movie from fifty years ago.

"Is this a new production? This script, I mean?"

"Yeah. Why?" He bends at the waist and straightens up and then twists from one side to the other and back again. It's like a fitness class being carried out in my living room.

"I was only wondering. The language is a little … stilted?" I can't help but wince when I say it since I don't want to hurt his feelings or anything like that. Granted, it's not like he wrote it, but this is clearly something that matters to him.

He rolls his eyes while twisting. "It's satire. It's supposed to be stilted to make fun of the movies that used actual language like that and meant it for real."

"Oh, okay! That's something I didn't know. Thanks for setting me straight."

Note to self: don't criticize the script anymore.

"Do I … have to prepare?" I ask when he starts doing lunges. Real, honest-to-goodness lunges.

"Nah. You're only feeding me lines. No worries." He finishes up with a heavy sigh, shaking himself out one more time. "I think I'm ready."

"Terrific. Where should I be?" I stand, holding my arms out to the sides in a shrug. "You tell me, and I'll do it."

He taps his chin, looking around the apartment

like he's never seen it before. "In the bedroom, I think. That's where the scene takes place. You can lie down like the girl does in the script. I'm the vampire who's just entered the room through the window."

Ooh. I can't even pretend this hasn't been a fantasy of mine. Not a frequent fantasy or anything like that. I don't make it a habit. But who hasn't imagined a sexy vampire slinking into the bedroom and seducing them until there's no choice but to succumb to the darkness?

I was super into vampires during the whole vampire book craze. I can admit it.

I slide out of my shoes before stretching out on the bed. Good thing I worked my butt off to get this place tidy. It's so much easier to know there aren't any embarrassing bits of laundry or clutter lying around. Less stressful than running around and kicking things under the bed when he's not looking.

He goes to the window meanwhile and positions himself near it. "When the scene opens, I've just entered. I expect this to go the way my nightly hunting used to go back in the day—before I got chained up in my coffin for four hundred years. I'm completely unaware of how savvy people are nowadays."

"Got it." That actually sounds like it might be fun. I rest my head on my folded arm and prop the script up in front of me. "Ready when you are."

It's fascinating how he changes. One second,

he's Rafe, the incredibly handsome and deeply artistic actor I'm currently dating. The next, he's somehow … taller? And thinner? *How did he do that? Did he suddenly melt off ten or twenty pounds? Am I imagining this?*

He moves like a cat, all smooth and graceful and dangerous, approaching the bed. "There she lies. The first true meal I'll get to enjoy over the course of these many centuries."

Oh boy.

"Awaken," he purrs as he draws nearer. "Awaken for me, my love. My prize. I shall savor you. I shall make you my own. We will rule the night together."

That's my cue. I prop myself up on my elbow. "Whoa. What are you doing here? Get the hell out of my bedroom!"

He recoils a little, and an entire range of emotions washes over his face all at once. It's hard not to laugh really. "What is this?"

"Didn't you hear me? Get out! Now!" I sit upright, checking the script as I do. "Go, get out. I'm calling the cops."

"You shall not. Look at me."

I pretend to hold a phone to my ear. "Nine-one-one? A pervert in a cape is in my bedroom." I snort a little at that one. I can't help it. I'm only human.

His chest puffs out before he raises his voice. "Look into my eyes, mortal woman!"

"Get the hell away from me! This isn't Transylvania, you sicko." According to the script, I'm supposed to jump up and grab a bat from next to the bed. I pretend to grip it in one hand while holding the script in the other. "I still hold the record on my college softball team for home runs in a single season, shit for brains."

Shit for brains? I mean, really? Somebody greenlit this script?

And my genre gets laughed at?

I take a pretend swing, and he jumps back, toward the window. There's actual fear in his eyes, in the way his lips pull back from his teeth in a grimace. I guess that gives me extra confidence.

"Get out of here before I cave in your skull!" I scream, waving my invisible bat.

"Kitty!"

Rafe and I both turn to find a tall, brown-haired, shirtless, barefoot man rushing into my bedroom. It takes a second for me to register it's Matt, looking frantic and out of breath, soon followed by a barking, galloping Phoebe.

Who promptly launches herself at Rafe and knocks him flat on his back.

"No, no, Phoebe!" I try in vain to pull her off Rafe, but all I manage to do is knock my nightstand over. The lamp crashes to the floor along with my alarm clock and the books that used to be stacked next to it.

"What the hell is going on in here?" Matt demands, going to Phoebe and dragging her away from Rafe. "Phoebe, sit. Calm down."

"Why don't you try calming down?" Rafe scrambles to his feet, red-faced and panting. "Fuck, we were running lines here. For my audition."

"It's true," I add when Matt scowls. "I'm sorry that we upset you or made you think … whatever you were thinking."

Matt's still a little winded when he whirls on me. "Whatever I was thinking? You were screaming about calling nine-one-one and caving in somebody's skull! You know how easy it is for me to hear everything going on in here!"

"What are you doing with your time, man?" Rafe demands. "Listening with your ear at the wall? Get a life."

"I don't remember asking you a damn thing," Matt growls. Phoebe growls too.

"Okay, okay, let's all settle down." I step between them, my eyes on Matt. "Thank you for coming over, but everything's fine. I'm sorry you got upset."

"How about being sorry for upsetting me in the first place and then acting like I'm fucking crazy for running over to help you get a psycho out of your apartment? How about that?"

"Don't talk to her that way," Rafe warns from behind me.

"Once again, wasn't talking to you," Matt snarls.

Even though his chest is bare, I put my hands on it to hold him steady. Not that I could hold him in place if he were good and determined to get past me. I'm not an idiot.

At least it seems to be enough to keep him still.

"I'm sorry. I'm really sorry. I didn't think."

He looks down at me, and for some reason, it seems like his eyes have darkened. They're nearly black, thanks to how his pupils have dilated. "No. You didn't think. You never think. That's half the problem." He takes Phoebe by the collar and guides her from the room, muttering and shaking his head the whole time.

"Wait a second. What's that supposed to mean?" I should hang back and pick up my things and make sure Rafe isn't hurt and all that, but I don't particularly enjoy Matt's little attitude.

"Forget it," he grumbles over his shoulder. "Go back to your whatever that was. Next time I hear you screaming bloody murder over here, I'll remember not to run over to help."

"Matt, come on."

But he won't listen. Instead, he closes my front door with a decisive slam and then slams his own door a moment later.

Wonderful. This is exactly what I needed in my life. An angry neighbor. Another angry ... *friend?*

Rafe is still scowling when he joins me in the living room. "What's his problem? I didn't love the way he was talking to you."

"It's complicated. We're friends. Sort of." I let out a long sigh, folding my hands on top of my head while staring at the front door. "I thought we were anyway."

Now? I have no idea. And the fact that having no idea makes me feel so sad and slightly sick to my stomach is only making things worse.

"Maybe we should run lines more quietly next time," Rafe suggests as he loops an arm around my waist.

I can't bring myself to tell him how little I care about his audition right now.

Instead, I force a tiny smile. "Yeah, let's keep that in mind. And let's clean up the mess in my room while we're at it." At least that's a mess I have some semblance of control over.

Unlike the rest of my life.

Chapter Eighteen

"SEE WHAT HE does there?" Rafe interrupts the movie we're watching on my laptop to point to the screen. "He's totally calm on the outside, except for the way he keeps playing with the napkin. You might not even notice it, being so close to the bottom of the frame, but he does it anyway. Because that's what his character needs to do."

I can't help but wonder if he ever watches a movie just to enjoy the movie, but I guess it's a lot like a writer reading for pure pleasure. I know I haven't been able to do anything of the sort in years. Not when I keep noticing small details the author added, turns of phrase I wish I'd come up with, all that.

"That's really fascinating," I murmur, which I wish I'd recorded myself saying so I could play it again and again. I mean, I've said it at least ten times already. I don't know how else to say it though.

Yes, I find this interesting. But I just want to watch the movie without half the dialogue being drowned out by explanation.

I shouldn't complain. We're on the sofa, Rafe spooning me from behind. I could think of a hundred worse places to be than lying here with his arms around me and my head resting on his bicep.

Still though, if I'm going to miss half the movie, I'd rather it be because his arms were around me and he couldn't resist my butt being up against his—

"And see?" he asks, pointing again. "That look. He said a mouthful with just a simple look."

"He did," I agree.

It's cute, right? That he can't quiet down long enough to enjoy what we're watching?

It's rare that I settle down to watch a movie, and when I do, I like to be able to concentrate on what's happening on-screen. That's not his fault though.

"Just think"—I snuggle in closer to him—"you'll be that guy one day. Somebody will watch you and look at all the little nuances in your performance and talk about what a genius you are."

"A genius?" He snorts close to my ear before planting a tiny kiss there. "I doubt it."

"I don't. I think you have what it takes. I really do."

"You're just saying that."

"Hey. I'm not." I have to crane my neck to get a good look at him, but I manage. "You're going to be a big star. I feel it in my bones. And I'll be cheering you on."

That earns me a kiss.

"I believe you would too."

"It's what I'm here for," I remind him, and he wraps me up tighter and nuzzles my neck. Hmm, I could go on like this forever so long as I keep getting smooched on. I close my eyes, sinking into the pleasant sensation of Rafe nibbling on my neck …

"Oh, this is my favorite part."

My eyes open.

Would it be wrong to growl? Or pout? Yeah, I guess it would.

"I didn't know you'd already seen this. You should've said something. I wouldn't have made you watch it again."

"Nah, I love it. I'd watch it a million more times," he assures me.

A million more times? This implies that he's already seen it a million times. I guess he gets slightly obsessed when he finds a performance worth interrupting what could turn into a hot-and-heavy make-out session … or more.

"Okay. So long as you're not bored," I sigh.

"Not at all." He inches closer, draping one leg over both of mine. "How could I be bored right now? With you all pressed up against me, making it tough to concentrate on anything else."

"Who's asking you to concentrate on anything else?" I ask, craning my neck again so I can see him. "There's not gonna be a quiz after the movie, you know."

One of his hands somehow finds my breast, which is not a bad thing, and his eyes narrow. "Good. I can relax and get to know you better."

"I wish you would," I whisper.

I really, really wish he would. Like, I'm dying over here. It's sweet torture, being in his arms with so much clothing between us when I've been lost in lust ever since the second I laid eyes on him.

He lowers his head, meeting my lips, and I could cry with joy.

Until …

"Oh, hang on. I love this scene." He nods to the screen, and now, I want to scream with disappointment.

How many times can he brush me off before I start to wonder if I'm the problem?

Just when I'm ready to give up hope of ever getting into his pants, there's a buzzing between us.

He slides his hand into his pocket and pulls out his phone. "Shit. It's Bill."

In a flash, he's sitting up while I lean over to pause the movie.

"Hey, Bill. What's up?" He's rattled. He's so rattled, the poor thing.

I know without being told that he's terrified this is going to be bad news. That he lost the audition or something like that.

As it turns out, the opposite is true. I can hear Bill loud and clear from my position right next to Rafe.

"They're moving your audition up to tomorrow, kid. We need to be on a plane in three hours."

"What?" He bolts up from the sofa, and I join him.

My heart's racing like I'm the one whose entire future rests on this audition.

"You'd better get moving. I'll pick you up in an hour, so we have time to get through security."

Rafe ends the call with shaking hands. "Um ... wow. Okay."

I loop my arms around his waist and squeeze tight. "You've got this. I know you've got this. And it's a good thing, right? Now, you don't have to wait a whole extra week. It would have been unbearable if you'd had to keep waiting and wondering. Now, you can get it over with. I know you'll be fantastic."

"I wish you could come with me and remind me of that before I go in," he admits before turning away from me to find his shoes. "God, I have to hurry. I can't believe he called and dropped that on me this way."

"I'm sure it's just as much a surprise for him as it is for you." I get his coat, and it occurs to me that my hands are shaking too. I'm just as nervous for him as he is. *But he needs me to be confident, to bolster him, right?*

"I'm not ready."

"You are. You know you are. I know you are. You're gonna kill this."

He puts on the coat, looking dazed, and all I can do is stand on my tiptoes to give him a kiss.

"You'll do great. Break a leg and all that. Or is that only for shows and not auditions?"

A real, true smile breaks through his mask of worry. "It doesn't matter. Knowing you care that much is all I need. Thank you." He wraps me in one big, tight hug and whispers in my ear, "And don't think I wasn't planning on taking you into the bedroom and tearing your clothes off. I was trying to be a gentleman."

Oh, how my heart sinks, but I think I manage to cover well. "When you get back," I growl, nipping his earlobe. "I might look like a nice girl, but I don't always want a gentleman."

"I'll keep that in mind." With one quick kiss, he's gone, on his way down the hall.

"Keep me posted, please!" I call out with my heart in my throat.

He's got this. I know he's got this.

But what if he doesn't? I can only imagine how devastated he'd be if he didn't get this role. After having read that tiny bit of the script, I have to wonder if it's even worth the effort, but it means the world to him.

And I can't be a snob like that. Haven't I already been hurt by snobs who didn't think my writing was any good because of my genre? It would make me a hypocrite to belittle anyone else's efforts.

I glance down at myself after closing the door.

"Well, at least I looked nice." Not that it got me anywhere.

How did Rafe ever get the idea that I wanted a gentleman? I mean, sure, that's great and everything. I wouldn't want to date a creep or a toxic alpha or what have you.

But for heaven's sake, a little time in bed wouldn't kill anybody.

Might as well take all my sexual frustration and pour it into my book. I close the movie since, to be honest, I didn't pick up on half of it between Rafe's constant interruptions and my general horniness, and I open my manuscript.

Things are going well for my hero and heroine at the moment. He scored a fantastic audition on the other side of the country—yes, yes, I know, stealing from real life—and she's joining him to offer support.

But things won't be so happy and cheerful soon because he's going to have his head turned by people courting him, trying to convince him to live the decadent Hollywood life.

Does that actually happen? I don't know. Maybe. Rafe might be able to offer insight when he comes back.

This is the point where the bonds my characters have created are tested. In their world, stupid distractions don't happen. They don't get interrupted by golden retrievers and phone calls. Wouldn't that be nice? They've had the opportunity to get to know each other on a physical level as well as an emotional one.

Rafe and I will have that chance. I'm sure of it.

Even though I can't help but wonder what will happen if he gets that movie.

Or if he doesn't.

Nothing like writing a graphic sex scene to forget one's troubles.

"Here we go," I murmur before launching into a scene in their hotel room.

Because writing about sex is just as good as actually having it, right?

Chapter Nineteen

I REALLY WISH Rafe would call. Or at least text.

The last thing I heard from him was his relief at making it to LA in one piece after the whirlwind he was on yesterday. And how he hoped he'd remembered to pack underwear. I reminded him they sold underwear in California.

Since then, radio silence. I don't know if that's a good thing or a bad thing. Maybe Bill's introducing him to all sorts of people. He's probably being courted by the producers of this movie, as gorgeous and charming as he is. I'm sure the second they set eyes on him, dollar signs started flashing in their minds.

And that's not just me being biased. Anybody with half a brain would jump on the chance to sign him to a movie. He'd look fantastic on a billboard.

Even if he's dressed like an old-timey vampire, I guess.

It's practically impossible for me to get any work done when I can't stop thinking about him though. My apartment's already clean as a whistle, so I can't distract myself with that. I don't have enough laundry to necessitate running a load. I could rearrange the books on my shelves, but I sort of like the way I have them right now—organized and separated by color, then by genre, and finally by author.

And it's raining and miserable outside, so going for a walk is out. It doesn't have to be out, but I've never understood why people wax romantic about walking in the rain. Who wants to walk around with their shoes all squishy?

I can't meet up with Hayley, and I still don't know what I'm going to do about that situation.

There's music coming from Matt's—just loud enough that I know it's playing, but not so loud that I know what he's listening to. I'm still a little miffed at him after that performance he gave yesterday— something I tried like heck to put out of my mind while Rafe was with me.

Now, there's nothing for me to do but stew over his attitude. I have half a mind to go across the hall and bang on his door, but it's only early afternoon now. He might still be working. I'm not completely thoughtless … the way he thinks I am.

What a freaking dick.

And the nerve of him! Telling me Hayley didn't mean the things she said when we fought. Then turning on me and telling me I never think. *What is that supposed to mean?*

Nobody asked him to be my protector. At least, I know I didn't. *What is going on with him? With*

Hayley? I'm not the person they're accusing me of. I need to get to the bottom of this.

When my phone rings, I practically jump on top of it like it's a grenade about to go off and I'm trying to save the lives of the people around me. Only there's no one around me.

And it isn't Rafe either.

But I'm just as breathless when I answer, as I would be if he were the one calling.

"Kitty?" Hayley sniffs. "I need you."

I'm on my way in a flash because it doesn't matter that we had a fight and haven't spoken since. My best friend needs me. I couldn't imagine holding a grudge right now.

Besides, I miss her. I'm glad she even thought to call me.

When I arrive at her place with a bag of liquor in one hand and a bag of junk food in the other, she's just as much of a mess as she sounded on the phone. She goes right to the couch after opening the door for me and burrows under a blanket. There's a box of tissues next to her, half-empty, and the balled-up tissues and chocolate wrappers around her tell me this is a serious situation.

I leave the bags for the moment in favor of joining her once my wet coat is off. "What happened?" I ask, sitting near her. When I'm up close, it's clear she's been crying for a while. I doubt anybody who knows her only as the dazzling, polished superstar would recognize her if they met her on the street in this condition.

"It was all wrong. I knew it was wrong, but I did it anyway. Maybe I was desperate to distract myself from the pressure. I don't know." She blows her nose, crying softly.

"I don't understand. What are you talking about, sweetie?"

"Tom," she blurts out before shooting me a guilty look. "My boss."

Oh. I sort of guessed it had to do with that, but the confirmation of my suspicions doesn't make me feel good. "I'm sorry. Oh no. Did you get caught?" There's a sick feeling in my stomach at the very thought.

She's worked so hard. Much too hard for things to go south like this.

She blows her nose again, and jeez Louise, I just want an answer. I'm dying over here.

Finally, she shakes her head, and I let out the breath I was holding.

"No," she manages in spite of her clogged nose, "I didn't get caught. But he did."

"Okay." Still not good. "He won't name names, will he? Can you trust him?"

She lets out a tiny whimper, shaking her head again. "You don't understand. He got caught with another one of the associates in my department."

"That son of a bitch."

"Can you believe it? He wasn't only sleeping with me. He was sleeping with Amber too. Amber!

Seriously, what?"

I don't know Amber, but I'm guessing she's not in Hayley's league. I mean, who is?

"Clearly, he's an idiot."

"Such an idiot." She twists the latest tissue in her hands, looking down at it while she does so. "I know this is going to sound stupid, but I actually thought … you know." She lifts a shoulder before her chin starts quivering again.

Which is approximately the time when my heart breaks. I didn't know she felt that way. I wish she had told me so in the first place instead of jumping down my throat. Now isn't the time to bring that up, however. Now's the time to show her I love her and never judged her for the choice she'd made.

"I am so sorry," I whisper as I pull her in for a hug. "He's not worth it, sweetie. You can do so much better, and you deserve so much better."

"What was I thinking?" she sobs. "Jeopardizing my career for him when he only wanted to get laid. That was it. A little fun, a diversion. I thought I was something special."

"You are something special. Don't ever forget that. You were special before you ever met that jerk, and you'll be special for always." I stroke her hair and maybe shed a tear or two. I've never seen her like this in all the years we've known each other.

"I'm so sorry for freaking out on you." Her tears are now soaking into my shirt, but I wouldn't pull away for anything.

"It's okay. I get it."

"It's not okay." She lifts her head and blows her nose again. If she doesn't cool it with that, she'll end up looking like Rudolph. "I was mean and cruel, and it was all because I knew you would tell me how sketchy it was for me to sleep with Tom. I knew it was wrong, but I went ahead with it. So, I tried to keep it a secret, but that made me feel even worse. I lashed out at you when I really should've been lashing out at myself."

"I get it," I tell her again, tucking her hair behind her ears with as much of a smile as I can manage while she's so upset. I can't help but feel for her—and goodness knows, she's nursed me through low times before.

"You didn't deserve it."

"Eh, sometimes, I can be dramatic and make a big deal out of things, but honestly, I was more hurt that you thought I'd judge you before you even gave me a chance to say anything."

"I know. I think I was caught up in all of the excitement and didn't want to face reality. I love you. I really do."

"I love you too. Let's not fight again, okay?"

"Okay."

"And take this whole situation as a reminder that you and all the hard work you've done are more important than any man. Ever. I don't care how hot he is."

"He isn't even all that hot." She buries her face

in her hands. "He's really not. And he wasn't that good in bed."

"So …"

"So, why did I sleep with him?" Her hands fall to her lap as she blows a long sigh through pursed lips. "I don't know. He's charming. He's smart. He made me feel valued—I know; I know. You think I'm awesome. But, Kitty, here's the thing: I work in a large firm with lots of people who graduated at the top of their classes. I'm a big fish in a pond full of bigger fish. It's easy to feel like I'm nothing special in the middle of all those fantastic, accomplished people."

"I never thought about it that way." I lean against her. She leans against me. "And you've been under a lot of pressure lately too. I can imagine how that would make you feel bad."

"Yeah, that has a lot to do with it too. I can't wait for next month. This will be over, for better or for worse."

"For better. I know your firm will win that case. You've done a lot of work on it. You're Hayley, the bright, shining star. You're brilliant. You wouldn't work with all those talented people if you weren't. I'm so proud to be your friend."

"I feel like such a piece of shit for ever saying those things to you when you're sweet like that."

"Good thing I'm not always sweet or else you'd feel bad all the time."

She giggles, which goes a long way toward making me feel like she'll be okay. "He lost his job."

"Good. He deserves it."

"So did she." She winces, turning to me. "Isn't that awful? That could've been me."

"I know, honey, but it wasn't. You had a close call. You'll know better next time."

"I definitely will. I decided to call out sick today to get over it, and then I'm moving on." She rests her head against my shoulder with a sigh. "What about you? What's happening with you?"

"Not much." Nothing that's happened recently is anything close to what she's going through.

"I know that's not true, so don't even play around. It's been almost two weeks since I last talked to you. Spill. Take my mind off my misery."

"Well, Matt's mad at me. Rafe went to LA at the last minute yesterday for an audition for a movie. I went to a writers group and got laughed at for writing romance." I shrug. "Same old, same old."

She eyes the bags on the floor. "I hope you brought enough supplies to get us through this."

Chapter Twenty

VODKA AND I are not friends anymore.

My stomach hurts.

Along with my head and just about everything else.

Hayley and I drank a lot of things. And ate a lot of things. And now, I'm pretty sure I won't make it home without puking. I'll be lucky if I make it through the front door after eating so much junk. Maybe I should grease myself to slide through.

Rafe would never have binged like that.

I wish he would call.

My feet are heavy as I take one slow step at a time. One … and then another …

Why are there so many stupid steps in this building? How in the world am I expected to climb them right now after I ate half my weight in cheese curls? Why is there no elevator?

Speaking of things that are wrong, why isn't Matt magically appearing in the hallway like he always does? Shouldn't he have been over here early this morning, apologizing for being a dick and embarrassing me? Or at least explaining what his little temper tantrum was all about?

Now that I actually wish I would run into him, he's nowhere to be found.

In all honesty, it's probably for the best. I'd end up saying something stupid, thanks to all the vodka. I've already made a huge fool of myself after drinking way too much. Something tells me that when Matt and I finally speak again, I'd better be clearheaded and able to hold my own.

Now is not that time.

I flop down on the sofa, throwing an arm over my face instead of doing the smart thing and getting a bottle of water. Hydration doesn't matter as much right now as lying here, trying to recover.

At least I have Hayley back, and by the time I left her apartment, it seemed that she might be on her way back to feeling like herself. Besides drinking and eating way too much, we did each other's nails—while sober, one of the only smart decisions either of us made today—and watched a few comedies to make us laugh.

Of course, I couldn't watch the movies without thinking about Rafe. Wondering about him.

Has he forgotten all about me so soon?

No. He's got a lot going on, and not hearing from him is probably a good thing. It means, people are talking to him, and exciting things might be happening.

If anything, hearing from him right away might've meant bad news. It doesn't take long to be rejected.

The ringing of my phone wakes me from a light, drunken sleep I didn't even know I had fallen into. I fumble with it after almost dropping it on the floor. My head is so cloudy. Like somebody stuffed it with … clouds.

It's not even Rafe either.

"Maggie." I close my eyes and wish I'd slept through the call. I'm not in the right mental space for this. Not with a row of martinis dancing the cancan in my skull.

"Kitty. You sound somewhat worse for the wear."

"How can you tell? All I said was your name."

"You sound tipsy. Not that I'm one to judge, but you do have a book to work on."

"It's coming. Really. But, hey, you don't even have me on the calendar yet," I whine.

"That's one of the reasons I called. You're all set. I'll need your first draft in a month."

"Wow, good thing I didn't slow down. How'd that happen?"

"Lois. She called and got you pushed through."

Huh, I guess she's still got it.

"She never called me back, so I'm a little surprised, but I'm very happy to hear the news," I admit, perking up.

"How's it going? Have you faced any challenges?"

"Nothing beyond the ordinary, so I'd say I'm

doing pretty well. My hero is auditioning for a big Hollywood movie."

A pause on her end. "Is your hero doing the same?"

"Yes. He is. How did you guess?"

"Well, isn't that exciting? What a terrific experience for him. I expect you to wring every last drop of information you can out of him when he gets back."

"I mean, it's not like I won't demand he give me all the details." I manage to sit up but immediately put my head in my palm. I really should've stopped with the vodka long before I did.

"Good. Make sure you put as many of them in the book as possible. The closer to true life you can get, the better."

She's said that to me so many times that I can mouth it along with her.

"Naturally."

"What about your social media? I see you've been showing your beautiful self there more often."

"Thank you for noticing. I'm doing everything I can. Did you know you can schedule posts in advance?"

Another pause in an otherwise short conversation. "Yes, I knew that. Who doesn't know that?"

"I didn't. Forgive me for being ignorant. Anyway, I set up a bunch of posts in advance, and it seems like they're getting responses."

"Have you been interacting with your fans?"

Oh, if only she knew.

"That's sort of a sticky spot. Yeah, I'm responding with positive things and what have you, but there's one fan in particular who probably isn't too happy with me right now. What am I supposed to do about that?"

"What did you do to her?"

"Nothing! Honestly. It's just that she already had a crush on ... my hero."

"Oh. I see."

"I met him through her."

"I got the picture. Don't worry about it." She laughs. "Honestly, nobody walks through life without at least one adversary."

"I don't know that I'd call her an—"

"Sour grapes are sour grapes. She'll get over it. Unless you think she'll find some way to tank your career because you're sleeping with the man she likes."

Right. Sleeping with. That's the ticket.

"No. I don't think so. I only wanted to get your opinion on whether you thought it was a big deal or not."

"I certainly do not. Anything else to discuss? Anything I should know about?"

Why do I feel like she knows something she's not telling me? It's that little hint of suspicion in her voice. Like she wonders if I'll share or not.

"No. I can't think of anything."

"So, you didn't tell three different would-be

authors to use your name on their cover letter while submitting to us? Without so much as going through an agent?"

"What?"

"Did I stutter?"

I can't think clearly enough right now to make sense of this. "Sorry, my brain needs to catch up. You're telling me three different people used my name on their cover letters? I don't even know any …"

Then, it hits me. "Oh, if they think I'm gonna let them get away with this, they have another thing coming."

"So, you did suggest this?"

"No! What, do you think I've lost my mind?"

"I wondered, to be honest."

"Maggie, I would never do anything like that. I don't even know those people, and I sure don't like them."

I do what I can to explain what happened, which the vodka isn't helping. And it's already all mixed up in the first place.

By the time I'm finished, I can practically smell the smoke coming out of her ears.

"Let me get this straight. They had the gall to laugh at you for writing some of the most popular romance to ever come out of this publishing house and then use your name as if it would improve their chances of being published?"

"I mean, without going to them and asking

straight-out? It looks that way."

"At least I know you haven't lost your mind."

"Not yet. I might be on my way but not yet."

"If you must find a group of writers to interact with, for God's sake, make sure they write romance!"

Her advice still rings in my ears after the call is over.

Leaving me with the question of whether or not I should reach out to Rafe. It's three hours earlier out there, sure, and I don't know what time his audition is supposed to take place. Maybe he only just got out of it.

Or maybe he doesn't care enough to include me in his celebration—or lack thereof. Maybe I don't mean that much to him. I couldn't even convince him to stop being a gentleman long enough to sleep with me.

When the phone rings again, I could just about weep with relief.

"Rafe. I thought you were dead."

"I'm alive, but I might be sleeping because this has to be a dream."

"Are you serious? Are you telling me—"

"I'm telling you, I got the job. They hired me. Bill's hammering out the details of my contract right now, but I got the part!"

"Oh my God!" I jump up off the sofa before thinking about it, which is a shame because, now, my head is spinning, and I'm pretty sure I'm going to fall over.

"I can't believe it. It's a dream come true. They loved me. They put us up in this great hotel, and everything today has been amazing and incredible, and I got the part!" He's practically floating on air in other words.

Aside from the fact that I think I'm going to be sick before this night is over, I couldn't possibly be happier.

"Kitty, this means I'm gonna have to be out here for a while. In fact, if things go well, Bill makes it sound like I'll be out here for a long time."

"Oh." I hit the sofa with a thud. "Right. I didn't think about that."

"I want you to move out here with me."

Yep, I'm definitely going to be sick. Like, right this very second.

"I've gotta go!" I manage before dropping the phone and running for the bathroom.

Probably not the way he expected me to react to his excitement.

Chapter Twenty-One

"So, HE WANTS me to move to LA with him since it looks like he'll be out there for a while. I'm pretty sure his agent only needed a foothold out there. He has one, so he's going to work his butt off to get Rafe more roles. For all I know, he'll never come back."

My grandmother has held her tongue throughout this story, which is probably some sort of record for her. I even paused at all the right places, thinking she would interject with her little quips or at least a sigh or two.

Nothing. Nothing but silence. For once, I want her advice, and she's glued her mouth shut.

"Well?" I finally break down and ask. "What do you think? Should I turn him down? This could be the opportunity for something incredible to happen."

"That it very well could be," she allows in a soft voice I know too well. The voice she uses when she has a whole wealth of opinions but doesn't want to say them out loud.

"Oh my gosh, if you don't tell me what you're

thinking right this very minute, I will lose what's left of my mind. Please. I'm begging you."

"You want to know what I'm thinking?"

"Yes, for the love of all that's holy."

Where the heck is Peter? He could be helping me. The woman woke up this morning and decided to keep her opinions to herself for the first time in my entire life.

She clears her throat. "I think you should do whatever it is you want most. What do you want to do?"

Ooh, she's good. What a typical Grandmother thing to say.

"No offense, but if I knew what I wanted to do, I wouldn't have come here to talk to you about it."

"Well, Kathryn." She sniffs, throwing her head back.

"I said, no offense, didn't I? I'm not trying to hurt your feelings." I sip my tea, which is delicious but not what the doctor ordered. Not when I'm still nursing what's left of a hangover.

Granted, if I hadn't puked last night—after making it to the bathroom, thank goodness—things would be much worse today. Throwing up wasn't fun, but it's made this morning a little easier to bear.

Still, I'm not feeling like sunshine and daisies at this moment.

My grandmother offers a sigh and a faint smile. "I asked you what you want to do because you are the only person who can make this decision. You know what you want regardless of whether or not you're ready to admit it."

"I really like him."

"I'm sure you do."

"And I can work from anywhere in the entire world. That's one of the great things about what I do for a living."

"Also a solid point." Her lips twitch a little, like she's trying not to smile. "Do you believe the two of you might have a future?"

"That's the thing. I don't know him well enough to answer that question. I'd like to think we could. But I don't know for sure."

I lean back on the couch, and for once, my grandmother doesn't scold me for having poor posture. "How will I ever truly know if I don't give us a chance to become something?"

"That's difficult. I understand why you would be conflicted on this."

"I don't want to lose what could be something great. He really is such a terrific person. I know you would like him even if he's an actor and you don't like actors."

"I never said I don't like actors."

"You did."

"I don't necessarily like an actor *for you*, my dear. There's a world of difference between the two. I've known an actor or two in my day in fact." Her eyes widen as she raises the teacup to her lips.

"I do not want to hear about it."

"You might find my experience enlightening."

"Somehow, I doubt it."

"I'll tell you anyway. While I enjoyed my time with them very much—more than I expected—that did not mean they were the right men for me. Every nice man in the world isn't necessarily the right man. Do you understand what I'm trying to say?"

"I think I do. But I don't have to like it."

She eyes me in her usual way, lifting one eyebrow. The woman might not be dressing as fancy as she used to, and the jewels are locked away, but she hasn't dropped that imperious attitude of hers. If anything, I'd worry about her if she did. Peter's a great influence on her, but he hasn't replaced her with a pod person … I hope.

"Can I ask you a question, dear?"

"I'd be concerned if you didn't."

"Sarcasm. How charming." She chuckles though, so she can't be too annoyed. "I want to know, if you were more serious about this Rafael person, would you go to Los Angeles?"

"If we were more serious, I would want to be with him."

"Naturally. But would you go?"

"How can I answer that question? It's completely hypothetical."

"There are no stakes involved here, Kathryn. Your answer won't change anything. It shouldn't be this difficult."

"But it is difficult."

"Why?"

"Because I honestly don't know. I don't even know if I wish we were more serious, to tell the truth."

"There's nothing wrong with that. And if your answer were no, why wouldn't you go?"

"Because I don't love him," I admit. "And even if I did, I wouldn't want to leave you."

"Now, now, don't use me as an excuse." I can tell it pleases her at least a little bit though. Her lips are twitching again. "You know Peter takes excellent care of me and would never let anything take place without alerting you immediately."

"It wouldn't be the same as being here though. I'd have to get on a plane and spend precious hours trying to get here. And I would hate myself the entire time for not being in New York." I wave an arm over the coffee table, where sandwiches and scones await. "And what would I do if I couldn't come here for lunch or tea on the regular? This is the best eating I do all week."

"I wouldn't like thinking I was holding you back, dear."

"You wouldn't be. I mean, it's not like you're the only person I would miss. I'd miss the heck out of Hayley. If she's going to make partner at her firm, it's not like she can float back and forth between New York and LA. And there's my apartment. I would miss my apartment. I'd miss living in the city too. I can't imagine being happy in Los Angeles. I'm not a West Coaster by any stretch of the imagination."

"For what it's worth, I can't imagine living out there either. Don't get me wrong. I enjoy the sunshine—within reason. I hardly need any help with the aging process, however, so I would more than likely spend most of my time indoors. I'm certain the dry climate would do my joints good."

"I do like sunshine," I muse. "But it's sunny here sometimes too."

"That it is."

"So, yeah, in the end, it's for the best that I stay here." I sigh, closing my eyes against a headache that won't let go.

"Drink some water, dear. It will help with your hangover."

I open one eye, feeling a little embarrassed and maybe more than a little annoyed. "How do you know I have a hangover?"

"My dear, I wasn't born yesterday. And while I don't intend to hurt your feelings, you've looked better."

"That totally doesn't hurt my feelings at all. Why would you think that?"

"Charming as ever, even with a hangover."

"Could you not make it sound like a moral failing on my part, please? I was drinking with Hayley because she had done something stupid and it almost blew up in her face and she needed to be cheered up. So, I brought over reinforcements, and we spent the day watching mindless comedies and eating our weight in food with zero health benefits."

"You're a good friend. Really, you are. I wish I had a friend like you in my life. All I have are hags, like that Whitney."

"Are you two on the outs? Again?"

Whitney has been my grandmother's frenemy for as long as I can remember. They've spent decades in the same social circles, so they can't avoid one another, but they're just as likely to snap at each other as they are to offer a backhanded compliment after giving air kisses.

"That is our normal state of being, let's not forget." She shrugs with a sigh. "My life isn't the same as yours, dear. You live a very authentic life. You are true to yourself."

"You think so?"

"I know it. Look at you. You carved a career for yourself in a very competitive genre."

My eyes widen.

"Oh, don't look so surprised." She snickers. "I know things. I might or might not have done a bit of research when you started off on your meteoric rise."

"Thank you."

"You are thoroughly yourself, my dear. No one tells you what to do or how to live. Granted, there are times in which I wish you would listen to advice—"

"There she is."

"But I wish I had a fraction of your self-assurance."

"Are you kidding?" That's enough to get me to sit up. "You're the most self-assured person I know. We've had this conversation before; I know we have. You're brave, and you know who you are."

"Even so"—she picks at a scone, frowning—"there are times when a person asks herself whether she's made the best decisions."

Darn it. I should've seen this coming. "Oh. Oh no, she didn't."

"Kathryn, it's—"

"Do you mean to tell me Whitney—that withered, old biddy—had the unmitigated gall to question your life choices? I mean, has she looked in a mirror lately?"

"Kathryn."

"She practically humped Jake Becker in the middle of your birthday party, and let's not even get started on the spectacle she made of herself at the charity auction. She tried to buy one of the firefighters off the girl who'd won him."

"You know she behaves that way when she's … breathing air," Grandmother murmurs.

I drop my voice to a whisper. "So, what did that crone say? That it's not cool for you to be with Peter?"

"It doesn't matter."

Now, even more pieces of an ugly puzzle are

falling into place. "Where is he? Why hasn't he at least stopped in to say hello? Everything was already waiting here when I arrived. What gives?"

She folds her hands in her lap. "He believed it best to make himself scarce for a while. Only a short while, mind you. He stayed long enough to prepare our tea and leave food for me in the kitchen. A few days' worth."

"Oh my God! We have to go get him!"

"Kathryn, really."

"What actually happened? Because I know he wouldn't up and walk out for no reason. He loves you."

"Be that as it may, Whitney had more than a few strong opinions when she paid a visit yesterday. It seems she was unaware of my relationship with Peter, and ..."

"You don't need to tell me anything else. I've heard enough. Where is he?" I'm on my feet, getting my things together.

"He said he would take a room at The St. Regis. It seems he's saved most of what I've paid him over the years, so ..."

"Good. Let's go."

Her eyes are roughly the size of dinner plates by now. "Oh, my dear—"

"Up, woman. We're going to get him and bring him home." *Why are there tears in my eyes? Why is my voice all thick and trembly?* "He loves you, and you love him. He's been a heck of a lot better to you than that stupid, vulgar Whitney could ever be."

There are tears in her eyes, too, and I can see she's barely holding on. This whole time, I've been prattling on about myself while her heart's been breaking.

"He felt he was ruining my position. He has a great deal of pride, Kathryn. He wouldn't stay here if he believed our relationship to be the cause of any pain for me."

"Is it?" I crouch in front of her, searching her face for any signs of the truth. "Is it the cause of pain for you? Or is he the first thing that's made you really and truly happy in years? Is he the one who took care of you when you were sick—every time you've been sick? Is he the one who's been by your side every day for thirty-four years? Is he the reason you look younger and happier and more at ease than I've ever seen you?"

"You know he is," she whispers before a tear rolls down her cheek.

"And did you want him to go?"

She doesn't hesitate. "Heavens, no."

"We're going. I'll get a car." I'm already on my phone, scrolling through the app. "Put your face on or whatever you have to do, but make it fast."

Within twenty minutes, we're pulling up in front of the hotel. Funny how we were just here not that long ago for the bachelor auction. It seems like a lifetime ago, considering everything that's happened since then—including Grandmother's heart attack.

Peter is on the fifth floor. I wouldn't normally go up to the room with her, but I don't trust her to go through with this unless I'm nudging her along.

"I'm certain he'll be humiliated," she whispers in the elevator.

"He'll be too happy to see you to feel anything but relieved you came to get him," I promise.

I know how he feels about her. I've seen the way he smiles whenever they're anywhere near each other.

Damn that Whitney for getting in their way. She's lucky I don't have her phone number.

"Are you sure this is the right course of action?"

The elevator comes to a stop moments before the doors slide open.

Which brings us face-to-face with none other than Peter, who's holding a suitcase in one hand.

"Peter." I step aside to make room for him and try like heck not to burst into tears at the way he looks at my grandmother. "We came to bring you home."

"Did you?" He looks at her, still standing outside the elevator like he's not sure he should get on.

She nods and holds out one hand. "We did. You've been away long enough."

"I've been away for two hours."

"Which is already too long. Unless you were planning on going to a new hotel"—she eyes his suitcase—"it seems you were of the same opinion.

Peter, I don't care what Whitney thinks. I don't care what anyone thinks—except Kathryn perhaps. And she demanded you come home, where you belong. Who am I to argue that?"

"So long as you truly want me to come back."

"I truly do. Please. You belong with me, at home."

He reaches out and takes her hand, and then he steps onto the elevator car with us. They stay that way the whole ride down to the lobby, holding hands and leaning against each other.

Chapter Twenty-Two

IT'S FRIDAY BY the time Rafe has a free minute to spend with me. He spent another two days in LA, essentially quitting his bartending job after disappearing for three days with no warning, and he has been packing up his tiny apartment in the meantime.

I offered to help, but he reminded me of the apartment's lack of space. Then, he sent a picture to prove it. Honestly, there would barely be room for the two of us to pack at one time.

No wonder we've only ever hung out at my place.

Now, there's nothing for him to do but say good-bye to his friends. They're having a party for him at Jonah's later.

Which only makes me feel like garbage since I know what I'm about to say, and I hate to think of sending him off to a party after it.

But it has to be done.

The fact is, I can't stop thinking back to what happened with Grandmother and Peter. That's love, what they have. The sort of love that makes a person sacrifice for the other person even if that sacrifice makes them unhappy.

I've never known that kind of love. And I can't uproot my entire life on the bare chance it might exist between me and, let's face it, a stranger.

Rafe's sure not feeling like a stranger when he shows up, throwing his arms around me and kissing me hard, passionately, as soon as there's enough room for him to get through the door.

And for a second or two, heaven help me, I want to give in. I want to lose myself in this happy moment. My man is back with me. He's triumphant, and he's on the cusp of something great.

It doesn't help that the slightest touch from him lights me up inside.

"Hey, take it easy," I manage between kisses.

He kicks the door closed and tightens his grip around my waist before lifting me off my feet.

Oh no. Of all the times for him to decide he wants to do it.

And once again, the devil on my shoulder tells me to be cool and go with it. We're both grown-ups, and hey, our entire relationship doesn't have to be predicated on whether or not I go to LA. There's such a thing as long-distance relationships too. There doesn't need to be a break-up tonight.

It's just that I'm almost entirely positive he'll take my saying no as a rejection, and he might wish he'd known before we took each other's clothes off.

As it turns out, I don't need to explain anything

once we reach the bedroom.

"You haven't packed anything."

"No, I haven't."

He goes from looking around the room to looking me in the eyes while he lowers me to my feet. "Why? Aren't you coming to LA?"

"I wish I could say I was, but I can't. I'm sorry, Rafe."

"I don't get it." He backs away, running his hands through his hair. "I thought you were coming."

"I never said I would. In fact, I threw up. The conversation sort of ended there. And this is the first time we've talked about it since then. I needed time to think."

"Let me get this straight." He smiles in disbelief. "You're actually not coming with me. For real."

"Rafe. I mean … you never gave me a chance to tell you I would. What, did you expect me to drop everything in a single week? To pack up my apartment and say good-bye to every one I know?"

"Honestly?"

"Yes."

"Of course I did. You're the first real, substantial person I've ever dated. I mean, you're on a whole other level." He folds his hands on top of his head, turning in a slow circle. "I was so sure you were the first right decision I'd made in my life. And what happened, like, right after we started dating? I got the audition. I figured that was a good omen. Like the universe saying, *Yeah, you two belong together.*"

I wish I could melt into the floor and never come back. "I'm so sorry. I had no idea you were so sure I was coming. I wouldn't have deliberately led you on. I didn't know, was all."

He's quiet for a long time, finally going to the living room windows and looking out. I give him his space, sitting at the kitchen island and watching for any sign that he's ready to talk. Silent minutes pass, where all he does is breathe deeply. His back and shoulders move in time, and occasionally, his fists clench and loosen.

"You're right."

My head snaps up in surprise. *Am I hearing things?* "I am?"

"Yeah. Everything was going so well, and I didn't stop to think of you. Your life. It was selfish, assuming you could live anywhere because you work from home."

"I know you weren't trying to be selfish. You were excited and got a little carried away. Nobody could blame you for that."

He turns his head enough to look back at me. "You're too nice, you know that? You could've laughed me out of this apartment just now, but you didn't."

"I can't imagine anybody ever doing that, especially to you." I get up and meet him in the middle of the room, where our arms slide around each other.

He rests his chin on top of my head. "I missed a real opportunity with you."

"You have a much bigger opportunity waiting for you on the other side of the country. It's everything you've been working for all this time. I'm so happy for you, Rafe. I really am."

"It won't be as sweet now, I have to admit."

"Oh, don't say that." I pull my head back to look up at him, and it pains me to see the sadness in his eyes. I had no idea he was so invested in my coming out to be with him. "Please. You'll have the entire world at your feet in no time. I'm sure of it. And pretty soon, you won't even remember me—or if you do, you'll know it was right for me to stay here. I wouldn't want to hold you back."

"You wouldn't."

"You say that now," I offer with a smile. "But that's the way it would be. You'll meet so many new people; you'll be part of this big, sparkly world. While I'm sure I'd look great on a red carpet, I know I wouldn't fit in out there."

"I can't say anything to change your mind?"

"You have no idea how hard I'm fighting to do the right thing," I confess with a soft, regretful laugh. "So, please, don't try to convince me. I know this is right. I don't have to like it."

"Okay."

Still, he takes my chin under one finger and tips my head back before planting one more gentle kiss against my mouth. It takes all the self-control I possess to keep from grabbing him and clinging to him like one giant suction cup.

Not the sexiest image I've ever come up with and one that makes me consider whether I should really be writing romance for a living. But I'm not feeling sexy right now. I'm feeling sad and maybe a little bit desperate, wishing like anything there was a way for us to be together without holding the other back.

"I'll miss you." He touches his forehead to mine. "Thank you for believing in me."

"You'll always have a huge fan here. Remember that. And if you ever decide to come back, you know where to find me. Right here on the Upper West Side."

That gets him laughing at least. "I'll look for your name at the top of the *Times* Best Sellers list."

"Very funny." Though it wouldn't be the worst thing if he found me there.

"And by the way"—he stops and turns toward me once he reaches the hall—"I'll see your name there again. I know I will. And I'll be celebrating with you. And if those awful assholes in that writing group see your name, that would be pretty cool."

"After three of them tried to use my name to get in with my publisher, I'll go over there personally and shove the paper in their faces."

"Do me a favor and record that, okay?" One more kiss against my forehead, one that lingers longer than it needs to, and he backs away. "Bye. Take care of yourself."

"You take care of yourself out there," I whisper since I can't manage anything louder with this massive lump in my throat.

I almost hate to think of a good, pure soul like him going out to Hollywood. I hope it doesn't change him because I like the man he is. I like him a whole lot.

My first draft is waiting on the open laptop, only needing an ending now. I already know how it's going to wrap up. I always have. It's just a matter of getting the words out.

That, and I couldn't stand writing a happy ending before my talk with Rafe. I always knew how that was going to wrap up too.

Now, it's got to be done. I've got to finish this project and put it aside. If there's anything positive about dating these random men and losing them one by one, it's being able to pour everything into the work and gaining closure once I'm finished.

"I didn't think you'd come."

She stood there, looking like an angel in her white dress, though it didn't matter what color she wore. Fiona would always be an angel in his eyes—never more so than now, when she was only a few feet from him.

"I couldn't stay away," she admitted with a tiny smile. "I hope I haven't lost the opportunity to be with you. I don't know if this life is worth living without you in it. Honestly, I can't remember how I lived before you

walked into my acting class."

"I'm sure you did fine on your own." What was he doing? Trying to talk her out of it?

The thing was, he could deliver any monologue with ease. He could convey any emotion. He could even cry on cue.

But he couldn't come up with the words to tell Fiona what she needed to know. What he hadn't been able to tell her back in New York, what had been in his heart every minute since he left her there.

Her expression didn't shift. *"I did okay, but okay isn't enough. You make me shine. You help me thrive. You bring me joy. You're who I want, and it doesn't matter which coast we're on. So long as I'm with you."*

His heart swelled as he reached for her, drawing her into his arms. *"God, I've missed you. And I adore you. Fiona, I love you so much. Don't ever leave me again."*

"To be fair, you left me." She was smiling when she pulled back to look up at him. *"You'll never get rid of me again, just so you know."*

"I'm okay with that."

It's totally cool to write through tears, right?
Cool or not, that's what I'm doing.
I really hope Rafe is happy out there.

Chapter Twenty-Three

I CLICK *SEND*, and my first draft is off to Maggie.

The Valentine heart box of chocolates sitting next to me is empty. *Why do they put them out so early?* Figures. Another Valentine's Day alone, and now, I have no more chocolate to drown my sorrows in.

I'm starting to rethink my decision to send Rafe away. Even if long-distance, I could have had a boyfriend to share this day with. I know it's the right decision, but do you know how hard it is to have a last name like Valentine and not actually have a Valentine?

At least Hayley is on her way over. We're going to have drinks and watch sappy romantic comedies.

I hope she remembers to bring chocolate.

I'm fixing drinks when she bursts through the door.

"Happy Valentine's Day, bestie!"

"Happy Valentine's Day," I cheer back, hugging her and taking the bag she's holding.

I'm so glad to have her back to her old self. She's obviously not working till all hours of the night now that her fling with Tom is over, and I get to talk to her more often. Of course, just when that happened, I had the inspiration to finish my latest book, but that's what makes us best friends—we understand each other's drive to be successful.

"I brought all the good stuff. Chocolates, of course, and all the fixings for our love-potion martinis!"

"Love potion?"

"Oh, yes. I'm serious. No more flings. I want to find a real boyfriend this time, and if drinking a few love potions makes it happen, I'm all for it."

I laugh along with her, but in the back of my mind, I hope they actually work. I've been with so many guys lately, but none of them have stuck. None of them were the real deal. They were just a means to an end. I think Grandmother's words are starting to settle in. I deserve more. I want more.

Just as we curl up on the couch to watch the first movie, there's a scratch at the door.

Phoebe.

"What's that?" Hayley asks.

"Phoebe. She must have gotten out of Matt's apartment again. Hang on. Let me get her."

When I open the door, Matt is standing there with a box of chocolates in hand and Phoebe sitting beside him, wearing a red bow.

"Well, hello, sweetheart. Did you bring me chocolates?"

"Uh-hmm, these are from me. Consider it a

peace offering. Phoebe talked me into it. She said she missed you." He peers over my shoulder when Hayley comes to stand behind me.

"What's all this?" she asks.

"Oh, Matt and I had a little misunderstanding last week, and he thinks he can make up for it with a box of chocolates."

"Aw, that's sweet," Hayley coos, tossing her hair over her shoulder.

Is she flirting with him?

"Am I interrupting something? Where's Man Bun? I thought he'd be here."

"If you thought *Rafe* would be here, why did you knock?"

"Honestly, your room sounded pretty quiet, so I thought I'd take a chance."

"Mmhmm. Sure. Let's say I believe you and accept your apology, so we can get back to our girls' night."

"Girls' night, huh? So, we can't stay?"

"Well, Phoebe can because she's a girl and could probably use some time away from you."

"Ouch."

"Fine. Come in. I'm not heartless." I take the box of chocolates from him and open the door wider to let him in.

Phoebe immediately jumps onto the couch and curls up in the corner.

"Here. Have a love potion," Hayley says, holding out a martini glass filled with a bright red concoction.

"Is this real?" Matt asks.

"I'm hoping so. I'm looking for a new man." Hayley winks.

She's totally flirting with him.

I try to change the subject, so we can stop talking about love potions.

"We're about to watch a movie. It's romantic and sappy and girlie. Can you sit and behave and not make snarky comments?"

"I'll try my best, but can I talk to you privately for a minute?" Matt has a weird look on his face and turns toward the kitchen.

He leans against the counter, so we're more face-to-face.

"Listen, Kitty, I'm sorry I haven't been around. I made an ass of myself that day. I shouldn't have freaked out."

"It was sort of nice of you to do that," I admit. "You thought I was being attacked, and you came to help me. I should've thanked you, but everything was so crazy. I couldn't think straight. And I thought Phoebe was going to eat Rafe's face."

"She would have, if it meant protecting you," he murmurs.

"Thank you. Really. And thank you for the chocolates. So, what's happening? Why are you bringing your neighbor chocolates on Valentine's Day instead of your girlfriend?"

"I'm living the single life again." He takes a

deep breath, staring at the floor.

I guess that explains Phoebe not needing to spend the night with me. "I'm sorry. What happened?"

"It didn't work out. You should know how that goes by now."

"Gee, thanks."

"Sorry. I can't control myself sometimes. I have days of comebacks all stored up inside."

"I guess I can allow that since you brought me chocolates. You know the way to a girl's heart." I don't even mind that much. It's easier, being friends than not. I won't feel the need to avoid him anymore, practically sneaking in and out of the apartment to keep from running into him. That's sort of a pain after a while.

"So ... you didn't answer my question about Man Bun."

"He's in LA. He got a movie role out there."

"No shit! Wow. Good for him. When's he coming back?"

"I don't think he is. I think he'll stay out there. I told you, he has what it takes." I shrug when his brows lift.

"And how do you feel about that?"

"I feel like he'll be a big star, and I'll hopefully make a lot of money from the book I wrote about him. What do you want me to say?"

"You seem to be taking it well anyway."

"It is what it is. He asked me to go out there

with him, you know."

He purses his lips, brows up around his hairline. "He did? And you're still here?"

"Of course I am. I have too many things and people here. I wouldn't want to leave Phoebe, for instance. I was afraid of what would happen to her if you spaced out and started leaving her alone overnight again."

"Yeah. She would miss you. We had a long talk about it the other day. She was pretty serious."

"I guess I need to stick around then."

We share a smile.

"What's up with Hayley?" he asks, pointing to the couch.

"Oh, right. We never talked about that. Turns out, the dude she was sleeping with was sleeping with somebody else in the department, and they ended up getting caught and fired."

His eyes fly open wide. "No shit! This is what I miss when I skip too much time with you. Damn. What happened?"

"I'll have to fill you in later, but let's just say, the old Hayley is back, and I couldn't be happier. Now, come on. Let's watch the movie."

Matt and I walk back out to where Hayley is snuggled up next to Phoebe.

"What took you guys so long in there? I was feeling neglected."

"I just wanted to apologize to Kitty and make sure we were all good."

"And we are," I add. "Now, who needs another drink before we get started?"

Hayley raises her glass, and I fix another love potion.

Once we have our drinks, Hayley pipes up, "We need to toast. To finding love."

"To finding love," Matt and I reply in unison.

Phoebe barks and moves to the chair while we smoosh in together on the couch, so we can all see the laptop screen.

This isn't turning out to be such a bad day after all. I'm right where I belong. In New York, between my two best friends.

Happy Valentine's Day, Kitty Valentine!

ABOUT THE AUTHOR

Jillian Dodd is the *USA Today* best-selling author of more than thirty novels.

She writes fun romances with characters her readers fall in love with—from the boy next door in the *That Boy* trilogy to the daughter of a famous actress in *The Keatyn Chronicles* to a spy who might save the world in the *Spy Girl* series.

She adores writing big fat happily ever afters, wears a lot of pink, buys too many shoes, loves to travel, and is distracted by anything covered in glitter.